# COMA

SEMIOTEXT(E) NATIVE AGENTS SERIES

This edition Semiotext(e) © 2010
Originally published by Mercure de France © 2006

Cet ouvrage, publié dans le cadre d'un programme d'aide à la publication, bénéficie du soutien financier du ministère des Affaires étrangères, du Service culturel de l'ambassade de France aux Etats-Unis, ainsi que de l'appui de FACE (French American Cultural Exchange).

This work, published as part of a program providing publication assistance, received financial support from the French Ministry of Foreign Affairs, the Cultural Services of the French Embassy in the United States and FACE (French American Cultural Exchange).

Published by Semiotext(e)
2007 Wilshire Blvd., Suite 427, Los Angeles, CA 90057
www.semiotexte.com

Special thanks to **Marc Lowenthal, Erik Morse and Alice Tassel.**

Cover art by Katia Santibañez, *Story of Red*, 2009.
Acrylic on wood, 20" x 20".
Courtesy of the artist and Jancar Gallery, LA.
Back Cover Photography: Catherine Hélie
Design: Hedi El Kholti
French Voices Logo designed by Serge Bloch

ISNB: 978-1-58435-089-7
Distributed by The MIT Press, Cambridge, Mass. and London, England
Printed in the United States of America

# COMA

**Pierre Guyotat**

Preface by Gary Indiana

Translated from the French and with
an afterword by Noura Wedell

*To Pierre Chopinaud*
*in the early years of an already beautiful life,*
*for his lively and wise assistance.*

*Many thanks to Diane Henneton,*
*Christophe Constantin, and Colette.*

# Guyotat's *Coma*

This bizarrely self-effacing and feverishly energized book has few antecedents: Genet's *The Thief's Journal,* Augustine's *Confessions,* certain texts that surpass and dissolve the stagecraft of self-presentation (i.e., Schreber's *Memoirs of My Nervous Illness*) with an insistent, pathological engorgement of narrative, a continual demolition of structural elements and distinctions between "I" and others, self and things, places, animals, trees: *Coma* reenacts the physical and psychic crisis Guyotat's writing drives him to, a crisis in which the production of language accompanies the depletion of the author's body, as if the means of writing were his fluids and secretions, continually exhausted and replenished in a febrile state; there is no surplus; Guyotat becomes the stylus and ink with which writing exudes from him, spatters across notebook pages, determined by a demonic economy: the needles of Kafka's torture loom and the body they mutilate are fused like Siamese twins.

The absurdity of memoir as a literary genre is obvious from its recent effulgence. Not simply because the conventional memoir is a tidy bundle of lies, crafted to market a particularized self in a world of commodities (complete with real or invented quirks, cosmeticized memories, failings that mask more important failings, self-exonerating treacheries, sins, crimes); behind its costume of authenticity lies the mercantile understanding that a manufactured self is another dead object of consumption, something assembled by a monadic robot, a "self" that constructs and sells itself by selecting promotional items from a grotesque menu of prefabricated self-parts.

The notion of identity this industrial process takes for granted is one that Guyotat explodes in each sentence. As with Genet's epiphany on the metro, Guyotat recognizes that he is *the same thing as the Other*, the same breathing pustule of snot, semen, piss, shit: this understanding of identity uncovers a truth too intolerable to franchise: that "I" is *nothing special*, and counts as nothing in the chaos of being it briefly occupies and disappears from.

Guyotat's abjection, like that of Simone Weil, is a desire for transcendence that necessarily constitutes a struggle against the body, against physiological need. If this hunger can't be satisfied (how could it?), the animal

hunger that chains us to contingency, to our coloniza-
tion by the social order, has to be ignored, despised to
the point of starvation. To nourish ourselves becomes an
obscenity if others starve; survival is obscene when the
organizing principle of existence is to *kill or be killed.*

*I torture because he tortures, he tortures because they tor-
ture*: Gombrowicz notes that savagery becomes "natural"
when practiced by all against all; the atrocities Guyotat
replicates in the texts that nearly annihilate him (*Tomb
for 500,000 Soldiers*; *Eden, Eden, Eden*; *Prostitution*, et
al.), the atrocities of Auschwitz and the Algerian War,
are the veritable human milieu of twenty-first-century
globalization, a regression that promises to fill everything
and kill everything.

In this situation, Guyotat's "novels" have a desperate
and desolate urgency: like Burroughs, Guyotat avoids
telling "stories" with escape hatches and oases of safety.
He shoves the implacable, documentary reality of the
present in our faces. Criticism typically relegates such
writing to the slum of science fiction, a specular future
that will never arrive—as if the state of emergency we
live in can forever be deflected by political delusions and
steadily higher doses of cultural morphine.

In Guyotat's case, criticism advises us to sample his
work in homeopathic doses, as if too much exposure
would kill us. In effect, Guyotat's writing operates as a

toxin that poisons what's valorized as literature, revealing its emptiness, its uselessness, its falsity. Guyotat spoils the flavor of bourgeois literary writing, like a drug that causes derangement of the senses. If we experience this as liberating rather than terrorizing, we realize the truth of Artaud's declaration that *all writing is pig shit*—an emetic scream that returns language to its original, primal function.

All writing is approximate, all language a substitution; Guyotat's is less distant from what it describes than what readers are conditioned to digest. If we literally can't stomach this language, we should be honest enough to admit it's not Guyotat's failure, but our defense mechanism at work, a deceit we practice in order not to go mad.

But in a reality turned upside down, to paraphrase Guy Debord, it is necessary to go mad to arrive at sanity. Guyotat undermines our relation to fixed ideas and a code of sentiments that literature has inscribed on us since the nineteenth century. This lubricant of the class system is a law of enclosures that invests emotion in accumulation and consumption. It should be the function of writing to expose this corruption of feeling—to destroy alienation, so far as that's even possible any longer. Guyotat is one of the few living writers who attempts this (Fernando Vallejo is another); if he liberally refers to the arduous effort involved, it's less a matter of egoism than a brittle assertion of fact. He doesn't confuse himself with Christ but identifies with what the social order treats as refuse. The journey of *Coma*, if it is one, is a progression towards the prelapsarian, a recovery of what we were before the Fall: something of the world instead of some exceptional thing in it.

This text, which eludes any category of literature, is an unexampled effusion of tenderness that can perhaps only be read through the prism of Guyotat's other texts: the author is present, an immolated "I" existing in what remains when the habitual comforts and distractions of false consciousness have been ripped away: "*a voice that tears off its bandages.*"

*Coma* erases time as diachrony. A horizontal text, as a comatose body is horizontal, its memories and perceptions available at the same moment. In this condition the torments of life no longer hurt us, we are free to remember what has happened to us without the pain of going on with things, and everything we have lost is present again.

A friend, who later died, fell into a coma for ten days after an operation; several friends gathered every day around his hospital bed, talked to him as if he were listening; they interpreted his nods and eye movements as evidence of his mute but entirely conscious participation in what I considered a *death-averse cocktail party*. I didn't believe what they told me (that he responded to jokes, for instance, or welcomed their embraces), though I know they believed it themselves.

Later, during four months when he was declared "cured" of the cancer that finally killed him, I explained that I didn't visit him in hospital because, if he couldn't talk *with* me, or communicate in some other, unmistakable way, I had to assume he was unconscious.

He said that, for those ten days, he was completely unaware of his surroundings or the people in his room; he didn't know he was in a hospital, until he woke from what he described as "a dream, with everything that happened in my life swimming through my mind, dead and living people both, *outside of time*"—this occurred five years ago. Six years earlier, when my mother became comatose, in a hospital in New Hampshire, six months before her death, she asked, through the veil of what was palpably a dream state, where my father was (my father had been dead for ten years), and begged me to call *her* mother (dead for thirty years). Guyotat's is the only book I know that convincingly elaborates this intermediate state between life and death.

The following narrative I have carried within me ever since, surfacing from a crisis that had led me to the brink of death, in the spring of 1982, I forced myself to speak again in my own name. At the time, I felt disgust—it was really the only feeling I could summon—in preparing and pronouncing the word "I" with my throat and mouth, since I hadn't recovered the totality of its attributes, and more—so much had I suffered in that journey. How write, then, how think about writing, deprived of an "I"? Ecclesiastes provided a model, and Job, for a future I did not see; *living, to live*; but then, restored enough to write it, would I not rather resume work on my figures— more real than myself—and increase their number?

In those moments when part of my claim to speech revisited my heart, and ever so slightly fractured my internal muteness, I saw, I heard this text, in normative language, as prayer, lament, a sweet bath of anger, improperia in the tone of Palestrina and Lassus, but addressed to *God*; still too close to the events to narrate them. For that, I would need to create new figures, to progress in shaping my language, and in understanding the world—and in laying myself bare before the affluence of others.

1

At the close of one of the last afternoons of the last
century of the millennium, I am with a friend,
Stephen, originally from Leeds and back from Hokkaido,
in the foyer of the Odéon Theater of Europe, waiting in
line for an exceptional performance by actors, dancers
and musicians from the villages of Peliatan and Abianbase
in Bali, Indonesia, descendants of those, from the Malay
Archipelago, whom Antonin Artaud saw in the summer
of 1931 at the Colonial Exposition in Vincennes.

I have just finished the first of my last three revisions
of the one thousand three hundred and fifty pages of the
whole of *Progénitures*.

In front of us, a tall girl with very long red hair and
a long black coat—hailing from the new East?

Seated in the second chamber of the red and gold hall, above and to the right of the stage, we see the show at an angle: profiles of bodies, objects, and instruments.

Fairly conversant with the stage, and participative by nature, I immediately begin to tremble for every artist, female and male, as I observe, between the moving drapes, the contemplation or voluntary casualness they exhibit before entering the stage. Before even attempting to imagine, for every last servant of the show, what constitutes his or her life, his or her ancestry, artistic training, mind and heart, I am less than him or her: and thus, in my fictions, do I make myself the servant of my figures, themselves servants each to another.

During the intermission—where, the girl from the East? might I find, afar, the woman that I lack, since I have decided, for *Tomb for 500,000 Soldiers*, a book that I intend to be subversive across the board, for more artistic efficiency (the female, woman, too *spent* on this issue), with the shadow of desire's double rising, monstrous within me (profitable for the work but not for life), to enslave the male—a highschool boy, tall, blue eyes, glasses buried in prolific brown locks, murmurs to me, in the rush to the foyer: "You have freed the imagination."

End of the show: outside, the light which has waned during the performance is golden and blue, it is bitterly cold: frost already everywhere.

With whom can I carnally partake of this "joy"—nothing compared to what I, as a Christian child, imagine for my life: to be torn apart by the lions, disemboweled by the bull, struck by the lightning of God; then adolescent, to be torn apart by brothels!—with whom can I share, now, so as to dissolve its fixity, this beginning of a beginning of a desired destiny, in the very neighborhood of the city where I have confronted it with a reality outside myself?

This path from the same to the same terrorizes me by its perfection! and even if the planet spun a thousand and one revolutions in between, the misery…

With whom then? the young woman has disappeared… Joy here below might consist in seduction and copulation with no pause, no end, no lessening of desire or pleasure; continuous fusion, or close to it—simply the cold space in which to pass from one being to another, but for what? My work is also a portrayal of that lack; and written in the language of that lack. And I work daily to explode that fatality.

Into movement, quick!

We pass a man selling manuscript poems, his own; I buy a leaflet, and, farther down the road, say to Stephen in English: *"That's me, really… that should be me."*

Just as I must transform my mother tongue if I am to translate my vision of the world into my fiction, if I am to make my figures appear and speak in it, I must translate everyday ideas, sentiments, intimate emotions in daily life into a language other than the national language; I must transform that speech into something more than simple speech: an emotion, an act, an event as to be found in the theater, in cinema, or in exemplary biographies; I must maintain the organic emotion of that speech—the emotion of the event—which borders on the ridiculous in regular language; in short, I must speak as one should speak, human to human (in my works, I need a foundational scene, slavery, to ensure the word's accomplishment), human to "God." As I refuse the everyday use of the verbal gift thriving in the work, and as I wish to remain similar to my fellow creatures, I sometimes dissimulate, beneath a foreign language with constructions and interjections taken from the theater or novels of that language, which I can also transform according to the requirements of expression, the speech, and emotion, that would designate me as out of the ordinary.

That man, about my age, coat worn to threads, hands shaking over his metered poetry, is myself if I was not myself. He is what the work I create and its social consequences hinder me from being. The work I create is undoubtedly within me and in my hands like a kind of intercession between me and the world or *God*.

I do not know whence issues the gift attributed to me, and which I've always considered an injustice. I do not know whence issues the strength to have it produce the work, I have never given myself any credit whatsoever, any will whatsoever.

Since I have only followed my own bent, exploited my natural inclinations, since I have never taken anyone as master but myself and our predecessors, since I have always worked within myself, without the least advice, all that surrounds, ennobles, constructs the little I feel myself to be—that nucleus, that quasi-embryonic origin (thought's first concern is origin), that embryo—is of a ghostly nature.

My truth is in that origin and not in what, of life, work, fame, or legend, has formed around it; perhaps it is in something prior to my birth, in my nonexistence (what is unborn rather than acquired). What counts is what I am, *before*; I don't care much for what comes after: human conception, birth, writing. In other words: nothing, or genes scattered into the world, or a god's intent.

I still cannot get used to the idea that talent—genius even—must be taken into account. What I add to the embryo is perhaps not of this world. Often, too often perhaps, the greatest actions of human history, the greatest works, the greatest discoveries—which I love and from which I garner strength—seem unworthy in regard to what I believe, with all my heart, man to be capable of.

2

Near the end of 1972, after the resounding closure of a two-year relationship with a woman, while working on the text of a show that is to be performed the following year, the transformation within me of writing into speech pushes me to the streets: the vision, in the Louxor cinema toilets in Barbès, during the intermission of *Satyricon*, of a very white, almost naked body, beaten by the soiled door and groped by so many coarse, brown hands, the vision renewed, of lines of men spilling out from the whore-houses of the Goutte-d'Or—the gold, the male seed of my reproducing whores—confirms my prenatal premonition.

A young child, I loiter on the other sidewalk, eyeing the hallway, from the street to the little garden behind our village hospital.

Later, from the other side, I watch other corridors, in working-class neighborhoods; children, with patched postwar clothing, are leaning against the opening, others play, fight, grapple in the dark.

We add François K. to the first provisional cast. When I meet him, a young aspiring actor, he is working on the renovation project of the large office buildings on rue La Boétie: homeless, he lives and sleeps there. We talk, he tells me where he comes from, tells me about his parents, his mother who manages the Économiques Troyens in Chaumont-sur-Marne, with his father who is also General de Gaulle's barber at the Boisserie.

Then, as if impelled to realize the Word on the spot, to follow the injunction of the text in the making, I ask him if he will undress, which he gracefully does among the large cans of paint, of sealant, the stepladders and the sheets of tarpaulin: his voice is drowned in inextinguishable childish grief, in saliva, snot, and tears.

The smell intensifies with his disrobing, which he carries out eye to eye, his to mine.

In the show, in its two versions, the first with several actors, the second with two, he is sitting, naked, center stage, on slaughterhouse refuse—which we pick in the morning on the premises: we must at times climb the heaps in order to grab the right horn, the right quarter beef, the one most dazzling—slopping off a cart with shafts raised.

Animal quarters, ribs, cartilage, horns, tails, pelages, bloodied coats.

He delivers the text in its entirety, with gentleness, violence, he growls it, clamors it, he sings it.

Much later, we occasionally live together. He writes, he draws, often with his own blood, at times, he scarifies his body. He offers me slashed, bloodied skin to caress, in the sweat of our embraces or our housework.

On certain winter nights, I park my van, an R.V. in which I am again living and working, in Barbès, beneath the elevated train, the back of the van jutting into the crosswalk. Our embraces take place with curtains drawn, on the open seat in the back, in the knocking of the crowd in the crosswalk.

One summer night, on rue Islettes, a shift in the crowd pulls us from the brazier around which we keep warm, with the girls, North African, and toward the bordello where, we embrace amid scuffles and cries under a red light: once separated, I feel a pang deep within my thigh, and outside, I see blood. It is a knife wound, whose scar will show beneath the blade of the nurse's scalpel, ten years later, as she prepares the stripping of my veins.

Twenty years later, François's degraded, bloated body will be burnt, incinerated at the Père-Lachaise cemetery.

Then, in March 1975, the defense of Mohamed Laïd Moussa, a young Algerian whom I met in the desert in 1968, a schoolteacher in a palm grove at the time, accused of murder in Marseille, the preparations for the trial, which I take on almost single-handedly, his murder after his release from jail, all reinforce my presence among his brothers in exile: before and following his death, at night after an offered meal, I often linger in those restaurants where, after closing, the chairs are sometimes gathered, tables pulled, and a singer appears to whom someone from the audience slips the name of a home douar, of a fiancée, for him to incorporate into his song. And each of them stuffs bills under the neckline of his shirt. Their exile is my own, in my own language. Sometimes the night ends on a mattress, in the back-kitchen, where the waiter, busboy, or cook, against me, under the covers, shows me pictures of his fiancée or of his very young wife and very small children.

It is in one of these places, where the owner refuses my money, that Noureddine first appears, nineteen, the Light of Religion, native of Adekar in Greater Kabylia, the only one I do not touch, because, though I don't know it at the time, he will later become, under his first name and then his last, the leading figure of my fictions, from *Samora Machel* to *Labyrinth* today: a whore at first, who is set free, and then a whore again, escorted from one bordello to the next, although he himself leads the way.

And thus, when I leave my work, I let myself be led by whomever I encounter, where they will. I take more pleasure in discovering lives, in peering under roofs— like Asmodeus, demon of sensuality and impure love, who bars anyone from approaching women—than in consuming pleasure, which is close to nothing compared to my writing, and yet which is intensified by the circumstances, the places, the bodies, ludicrous, sometimes dangerous.

Drugs come with love. One night, in a long studio in a northern city, around New Year's Eve 1976, a slice of a round cake decorated with thirty-six candles, my age at the time, passing from hand to hand, is offered from above; I eat it. I am almost immediately lifted from the ground, carried, arms grasping the armchair. I wake at noon, on the mattress (pallet) of an angel, one quite ballsy, a mattress from which myself and D., who is half my age, shall emerge three nights later, for food.

For a very long time, it is impossible for me to understand why this half does not always progress as half, in time: he, 20 when I am 40, 25 when I am 50...

(In the heat wave of the summer of 1976, a friend, J.-J. Abrahams, *The Man with the Recorder*, wanders around Paris, in his Citroën 2CV, with his son Yaweh, 7 years old, fed by the people in the streets.)

At night, in winter, back from his job as a night barman, Noureddine settles across from me as I work on my mattress, upright in his chair, immersed in his native aroma, cedar, cork, oak, juniper, smashed olives and benzoin, which the frost outside intensifies: he tells me the fireside stories his mountain grandmother has handed down. He is the one I would have liked to be, simple, subtle, and beautiful like Nature and commerce, with many children in his loins.

# 3

I n early March 1977, a friend, David, a painter and photographer, comes to my house: I am working on *Encore Plus Que la lutte des classes* (*EPQ*), a fiction of speech in which you hear the exasperated echo of mine, or that of others, spoken in the ghettos at night. For the past few weeks we have been planning a hitchhiking trip to Mount Athos, to Turkey, and to Asia.

At that point, I have traveled too much in my own van not to want to do so in the vehicle of others.

But the work is there, beneath my fingertips, the voices that I must set free from my guts. I want to postpone the trip. In front of my friend, the alternative erupts, the debate, an ancient one for me, between oeuvre and life.

The dilemma has lost its power since then: the more I intervene physically in language the more I feel alive; to transform language into Word is a voluntary act, a physical act.

There may perhaps be a debate between literature and life, but there is none between what I write and life; because what I do is life.

There is nothing worse for a person of will than to go back on a seasoned decision—here, this trip, the two of us, to the far end of China. All internal order is thrown into disarray.

The following afternoon, I lay against my neck—already weakened, its aorta showing—the blade of a small fish-shaped knife given me by my friend Agnes.

A passing Algerian friend grabs my arm.

That very night, my brother R. comes from Orléans, where he lives and works, to take me back there.

Settled into a corner of the living room, I resume work on a yellow notebook, filling its pages, the totality of their space, with references, chunks of writing as if embedded in the page.

I go forth in the sounds of the life I have just left, those of nights, back rooms, whorehouse corridors.

What I had but glimpsed previously, for some short hours, or perhaps days, in deserts, relationships, depression, now settles in me, severs all movement from my center: work, language, the composition of figures and places, the accentuation of each voice according to what it does, that alone sustains me near a world that now exists only for the five senses of others.

One evening, at the home of some friends of my brother's, with everyone eating without me at the other side of the living room, as I no longer can, the sound of forks, knives, and plates heightens the anxiety that keeps me prone and stiffens all my limbs.

Who? What? What shock will lift me from this mute terror?

Long ago, in one of my first trips to the movies after the war, 1947, before the main feature and after the "newsreel," so dark and frivolous then, there is a short that narrates the treatment and recovery of a man who is suffering from amnesia. In a large, somewhat dark room, like the ones in *The Gold Rush* or in *Greed*, dirty, lowceilinged and long (the hypnotized patient is lying fully clothed on an enclosed bed in the front left of the shot), therapists reconstruct the place and time of the onset of the lesion based on accounts of the man's friends and family (a soldier, perhaps back from the European or Asian front); in the right corner of the room, toward the back, a nurse is bending over a coal stove, frying some eggs: the oil in the pan starts to sizzle, the therapists clear away the pillows around the patient's ears, other sounds around him as well, louder and louder, more and more powerful, the patient—his leg starts to tremble, then his body, then his torso, finally, all sounds at a maximum—sits up and stretches his arms out in front of him. He answers questions about his immediate, then more and more distant, past...

After a political event, where the dust and slogans reinforce my distress, the decision is made to intern me.

# 4

My father's brother, Jean G., a well-known neuro-psychiatrist, takes me to Doctor Brisset's clinic in Ville-d'Avray, in the western part of Paris.

Doctor Brisset is very understanding, and takes my health and the work I am doing under consideration. My uncle tells him that I tried to hurt myself. They lead me to the upper floors, into a fairly vast room, but with low ceilings. With a small window, iron bars across it, closed shut (?), almost aligned with the floor. My uncle reassures me, but as he is leaving, with the nurse, I realize they are locking me up—there is a sort of vestibule—and that he has deceived me. The door is locked from the outside and I have no air. Summer air... They bring me food and, already, tranquilizers.

It is a civil internment, much more exacting than the military internment I endured long ago.

At the end of that afternoon or the following, the first visitors are my friends C. and J., in whose arms I weep: but a ladybug with seven spots spreads and gathers its elytra on C.'s naked shoulder.

Several days later, I am moved to a room on the second floor, giving onto a small white wooden balcony from which I hear the sounds of summer again, spacious, with higher ceilings, its furniture made of nice wood, a kind of desk takes up an entire corner on which, at night, in one of my jolted awakenings, I place the little yellow notebook. Every morning, a small, rotund, and happy nurse, the mother of many children no doubt, administers an Anafranil and a glucose drip.

Many visits in the afternoon. My family gets off at the train station at Sèvres-Ville-d'Avray and takes rue Riocreux—a place, and a family name, from our native region—near Balzac's *Maison des Jardies*, walks by the house in which Mehunin and his family lived before the war: at the bottom of the valley, Corot's ponds, which I copy as a child.

The clinic is built up on the hill, alongside the wall that encloses the parc de Saint-Cloud. A very steep double alley leads to the three-story, Norman-style building, with an attic, a pointed gable on the left, a terrace on the side with flowers and benches where the patients bring their visitors.

Doctor Brisset tells me about Jean Delay's book on Gide. In his absence, a small, deformed psychiatrist takes care of me. She reminds me of a Miss Lacloche, whom we call Clochette, who vacations with us long ago in my granduncle's house in Brittany: since her room opens onto a stoop leading to the sea, we assemble there when it is stormy and the tamarisks are flattened, sitting on the floor, she humpbacked in her wheelchair, to hear her tales of fairies who shrink humps and straighten limbs with a touch of the wand, and we watch her, and think she is the fairy bringing about our internal transformation.

I roll my cigarettes in a tobacco box on the terrace. I lend my cigarette roller to the "mental retards" among the patients, and they lick it with their thick doughy tongues. The traces of their drool on the fabric are for me the biblical scrolls, the roll of Ezekiel with words of saliva, saliva in the shape of words, saliva shining like words.

Once I am able to walk again without feeling dizzy, I go to the parc de Saint-Cloud.

*

At 19, in June 1959, I flee to Paris, then to Saint-Cloud. The flight from Paris comes after seeing my father at a crosswalk of the carrefour Médicis. He has come from our native village to fetch me. Racked with anxiety, I leave in the morning, taking a 9.5 mm secondhand movie camera bought in Lyon, and I shoot statues, plants, animals, insects, birds. I wait long stretches near burrows and holes, behind the entry, for the rabbit, the field mouse, the snake, I wait. I eat bread on benches. I have to save money for the room. I watch Paris from the large terrace: when I feel that my father has left the city, I return to Paris and find a job.

I am a messenger, on a moped, it is very hot, I wear a blazer. I make deliveries to wholesale retailers, I pick up dresses from garment makers. I work for a clothing boutique, boulevard Montparnasse. I go to get fabric, trimmings, buttons, ribbons from the wholesale retailers in the Temple district. I pick up dresses and garments from the seamstresses, at their homes, mostly in the suburbs. At the time, the only route from Paris to the suburbs follows the boulevards des Maréchaux. The suburbs are closer to Paris then than they are now. And the towns aren't cut through, torn apart by highways. In three weeks, under pressure, I get to know the streets of Paris and its suburbs. I enter people's homes at all times of the day. I see the labor of sewing, I again smell the scent of fabric, of thread, of sewing machines, of wet finish, of the seamstresses' hair as they bend over their work, their cleavage bared in the heat, the labor and the tending of children. I get to know the sometimes aggressive solidarity between tradespeople, between artisans. Again and again the smell, of the button and ribbon workshops. The artisans in the back of the courtyards. On rue Saint-Roch, a man and wife, owners of a button and umbrella shop, always invite me to stay for a while or offer me a glass of mint water, and at the end of August they offer me their daughter's hand in marriage.

Most thankless of all is delivering the dresses to the rich customers and to the large boutiques on the Champs-Elysées. Wealth and luxury reserved for the very few is, and remains, intolerable for me.

But in a suite of the Plaza Athénée on avenue Montaigne, I deliver a very beautiful dress to an American woman of a certain age, who spots me in the entrance and invites me in. Her jewelry tinkles. One thing leading to another, as she is unpacking the dress with the maid, we start speaking about William Faulkner, whom I am just discovering at the time, and whom she knows "pretty well": many whiskeys on the consoles and at the foot of sofas.

In the parc de Saint-Cloud I begin to acknowledge the loss of my mother. Prior to that, I am swept up in collective mourning; my flight to Paris, my isolation, becoming engaged in my own destiny, personalize the mourning. And it shall last forever. It is one of the only "absolutes" of human life: something that resists relativity. The same occurs with the loss of the father, although that mourning is as violent as this one is tender.

On the park benches and paths, my inner dialogue with her rises to my lips and we speak to each other softly in my voice. I am writing, at the time, in a small room in Passy, on rue Chernoviz (where the detective my father has hired will find me at the end of August, the very day I send my father a note), a text that I carry with me in the morning in the inside pocket of my jacket, and that I continue working on, during the day, in the jardin des Tuileries and in small suburban squares. Grief over her death mingles there with anxiety over the future. I feel my physical, athletic participation in that destiny, the shoulders, the feet… the intestinal strength it requires.

The pain of imagining, of knowing that my father is far away and lost in his triple grief, his own mother's lack of love, his mourning, and my absence (I send him only one telegram, from the Champs-Elysées on the morning of my arrival in Paris at the Gare de Lyon, to reassure him but also to signal my emancipation).

One evening as I am walking home along the Left Bank, grief urges me to throw myself with my typewriter, into the Seine, into its luminous water (the lights of the city like some great hostile unknown, contrary to my nature, and which I shall have to cross if I am to gain a true name…). Between l'Alma and the Champ-de-Mars, on the street that runs along the bank, a car passes on my right, pushes me to the left, and I fall in. I tear the shoulder of my blazer; a seamstress friend sews it back together the following day, in the northern suburbs.

At the time, with my family fare train pass, I get in the habit of taking trips on weekends. First to Charleville where I enter Arthur Rimbaud's childhood home, go up to the higher floors. At fourteen, when I first discover Rimbaud and a bit of his life in *Paris Match*, I imagine those native stairs, those landings like the ones in the building since destroyed, on the first floor of which is a post office and a printers' shop and above which is my father's medical office. That dark, cold stairwell, leading up to the attic where my brother and I share a room.

In Brest, on the heights overlooking the port. An Algerian man accosts me and closes in on me, in a small military building. I don't know what words I use—but the gentler they are (how can one act violently toward someone in exile?), the more the man grows insistent— I break free, he chases me, knocks me down, and pins me to the ground. At the sound of a voice, he jumps up and flees. That brutalization of my being, wounded and in absolute pain, intensifies what I have been resisting with the weapons of youth: the judgment of my father and of general authority; their truth is my mistake, my forfeiture.

I experience all pain (even physical pain) or adversity as compensation—and not "punishment"—for some cowardice or other that has not yet been "atoned for": but there is no morality in this, nothing but pure logic, pure material, one weight offsetting the other, the balance of Judgment...

*

Ville-d'Avray, July 1977: I walk with a name that is mine, one I no longer feel inside but which others return to me. Every afternoon, family and friends come to visit, bringing gifts. We talk on the terrace blooming with flowers.

But one late afternoon, on the terrace that is slowly drained of voices and footsteps, a friend and I listen to a bullfinch singing under the cover of the leaves. That light song, so stumbling, fragile, at times so soft, so tenuous it seems to come from the beyond, is the very one I attempt to compose before my depression, and that I do not wish to interrupt with travel. A song now prohibited, inaccessible. The word *bouvreuil* [bullfinch] itself, its roundness of breath and the trembling of the *u* and the *l*, such pleasure, such words are now forbidden to me: because of a judgment superior to morality, to Art. Inaccessible. *Physical* laws keep us apart. The ease of birds, the torment when depression removes you from the world: non-depression is winged feet, whatever the obstacles.

I return to my room for dinner, anxiety buckles my knees, the woman psychiatrist enters and leads me from the room, onto the landing, a kind of bow window (where we can hear the patients below and in their rooms masticating), sits me down before her and takes hold of my wrists and arms, then stands up, hugs me close, deformed... I get through dinner: that very night, in a flash of dreams that I try to endow with as much power as they possess in my moments of creation, I get up and take the yellow notebook from my backpack, spread it open upon the desk to the previous month's unfinished page. I have an apple, from Orléans, in that bag, I am hungry but dare not eat lest I disrupt the order that is taking hold within me; I would like to stay awake with that uncertain deliverance in my chest, have it linger there, but hunger lulls me back to sleep.

# 5

Down south, I settle, with my van, near the house of some dear friends, on a plateau with short shadows, and set to work immediately, transporting chairs and tables from one dip of shadow to another. The trip that I cancelled in the spring, I will take this summer, then others, on a larger scale. They will be live, on the typewriter.

Rid of depression, I can finally look at the world and forget myself. The scene that shall become *The Book* stretches to the dimensions of History. To flee Western geography. I write outside, pushing on until the onset of the winter chills, traveling back through humanity's past as the weather grows colder. As the sky and earth are transformed above my head and below my feet. At the time, I believe that to work outside is to deflect the return of depression. I work under a Sun that does not move and on a teetering, spinning Earth, I feel it—that is what I want to impart, in the language of what is becoming a book, the feeling of that rotation. I feel it strongly, I often see it in dreams as well: the curvature of the Earth, because of how I am placed, and where, I see the curvature of the Earth, in imaginary places as well, a kind of Hyperborea hailing from above Scandinavia, infinite, blue, scintillating, endless archipelagos, endless planet, endless world; extraterrestrial spaces are enclosed within the space of the Earth itself. In these visions, I see the curvature of the Earth at the end of a tilled field: the furrows drawn by Bruegel's sower follow the curvature, not of the hill, but of the Earth.

When writing, I settle into the central axis of the Earth, my existence, as a *humble plowman of language,* is grafted onto that axis, onto the axis of that movement, which is more grandiose than human movement alone: the movement of the planet: the rotation of the planet, with its sun and stars: and in this way to elude even the feeling of death.

To return to the horde, to return to humanity, to leave this gravitation, to return to this human atmosphere, is dangerous! I know very well that depression can swoop down on me again, and this time keep me longer.

By moving my campsite around, I change my ground; I change my historical direction. In the work at hand, I mine the very ground on which I settle. I walk, I wander with my friends, I imagine, in the ruins... Those ruins, upon my return, I restore them on the page, I transform the ruins of the Roman villa into a Roman villa.

Caught between that infinite, "above," and this research of origins "below" that has tormented me since childhood: objects, buildings, ideas; between two infinites to which others are adjoined.

Ever since, as a child, they show me a coelacanth, a fossil fish, our ancestor, upon its discovery, for a long time I envision the beginnings of human life as a fish jumping out of the water onto the beach, and getting by there, with its underwater organs: several minutes, before another leaps up beside it, and survives a while more.

The day that I am told about universal gravitation, that the Earth spins around the Sun, I understand, faster than I understand how to read a watch or a clock face, that others, humans, animals, are awake on the other side of the Earth while I sleep; that is to say, that one humanity watches over the one that is sleeping, and the sleeping one dreams of the other, awake.

The thought of History comes to me then, as a child, the thought of tomorrow, of how night divides yesterday from today: night is rumination on the future.

I see, then, History contained, great figures, treaties, celebrations, people communing, battles, in the blue sky, inside the firmament: the lofty dead, all the great thoughts, aligned above: the sky rustles with those actions, and at night, the stars signal each, every, all; Time is there, up above.

The more I move back in Time, the more I feel estranged from my "self"; but imagining and setting up that distant world requires the support of a "self" whose power is tenfold: to be that Roman, Greek, Persian, Egyptian, hierodule, or boat carpenter from the Cyclades, means to wrench a past "self" from one's "self" and have it live daily at one's side.

To imagine and convey the thoughts of a figure of the past simply through the materiality of gesture and secretions; not only the sentiments of that figure, but its soul, according to the knowledge and the historical circumstances of its time, and what I can imagine of its knowledge and experience.

Working at night and in the growing cold, by candle-light, I see stars above me enter into the text, into the pockets of an astrologer from northern India, according to Alexander. The snapping of a tree beside me is incorporated into the text, not as a tree snapping, but as the creaking of a boat, of a trireme, of a galley.

What historical abysses between two sentences, two words!

The hem of a Kshatriya's dress, trailing along the deck of a theater-boat on the Ganges, takes me half a day.

Using the figure of the priest, his sacred hierarchy, I delve back to the origins of the god he serves.

People that walk by, farmers toiling in the fields around mine, children, animals, they enter my pages, transformed in time and space. The voices of others inflect how a sequence is modulated: a young Gypsy girl parts the thickets at the top of the meadow where I am working, and throws me bouquets.

Sometimes, elsewhere, I drive down to the sea, set up my van, retarded adults emerge from a neighboring institution, run alongside the bus, to go swimming in the waves; emerging from the water, they congregate to talk, to shout around the van with its tailgate up, where I am working, reclining on my stomach like a Roman at dinner.

In those moments, any interruption of my work can interrupt the anticipated sequence of events, and in two or three words, displace the centuries or continents.

*

Near the end of the year 1978, back in Paris, working again in my narrow room on the rue de la Gaîté: the text revolves, in ancient Persia, around the rituals of Mazdaism. My wanderings in the text between good and evil, light and night, start to animate the angry masses in insurgent Iran.

The figure of the Ayatollah Khomeini, his turbaned head, and tall, cloaked body, occupies our eyes and dreams. His voice, nearly inaudible, in that restless face; that obstinate forehead, from which I feel the devil's horns might grow instead of those of Moses.

The figure of the religious judge, falsely tormented by the torments he inflicts, false priest because of wedlock; with the transformation that is incipient in my gaze, of light that seems to be enclosed by dark, of very hollow hollows, of very dark darks, the light blinding—past: night; future: day; no self between—that judgment, that anathema of the religious, confirmed in the cries of boundless masses spreading over almost all of that vast country, is the entire mechanism of judgment settling in, and whose exasperated shadows rise and come alive against the back wall of the room where I have my bed.

For me, the priest is, and remains, the one who can hear everything—and imagine everything—without any surprise, he is the messenger and ordainer of forgiveness; in what I write, what might I pit against this figure of cold vengeance: in the text parallel to *The Book*, written at night, more freely, in pencil on a notebook, a figure appears in the bordello: "Samora Machel," the whore, the Compassionate one, the Light of Night.

6

I n early spring 1979, before writing what shall become
the final scene of *The Book*: Nehemiah's wanderings,
around 445 B.C., along the ruined walls of Jerusalem in
order to rebuild them, I decide to renovate my room:
repair the ceiling, level the tiles.

Is it due to breathing toxic fumes, or to having interrupted my progress, through spaces, monuments and
peoples whose complete forms I restore, along with their
gestures and their souls; but in the middle of the season,
I am beset by profound weariness.

I go south again, to resume work, outside, beneath a tall
cedar tree, at the entrance to the property where a

painter friend of mine is renting several rooms to live and work.

I write the definitive version of the Nehemiah episode, under those branches where, come nightfall, an owl, the bird of wisdom, settles and makes its cry. Two visiting friends, who work in movie production, want me to set to work on an idea I submitted to my editor two years before—an edition of texts in progress that would be accompanied by an audio cassette—and record me, outside, reading several pages of this fake ending: my diction, soft, light, surprises them, disappoints—it is always expected that what I write, I must violently pronounce: an enchanting lament turned tragic ranting?

That very evening, in what little light remains, I resume, in my mobile dwelling, under the gas light, and in notebooks, the parallel work in progress: *Tales of Samora Machel*, where a whore named Samora Machel labors, and is labored. In order to unwind, in my own century, from the figures hailing from centuries before Christ.

Marseille, just after the war. In the intervals between sex during a test period on the pallet of his new master, the so-called Fanget, Samora Machel, long, large black curls, sixteen years of age, destined to a life of prostitution since his mother's belly in Lisbonne, recounts his life in Blida

(Algeria), at the "Roseau d'or," working for Lahcene, the latest in a line of owner-pimps.

Samora Machel is, at the time, the name of the revolutionary leader in Mozambique. Why has that name gravitated to my throat and my pen? Because Samora is the chest jutting out in front, the ass in back, and Machel is girl's hair, under which verbs and semen are masticated, along with other sense-sounds.

The pull of that name, of the forms and the temperament it contains, is such that the next day, at dawn, a summer dawn now, I take it up again to make it speak, question, appear and disappear, in embraces, acts of haggling, in the midst of laughter, and anger. The athletic text of *The Book*, that night, before what I foresee of my near future, gives way to a text that shall become, in the following eighteen months, through my internal and external battle through them, a comic-heroic lullaby of sorts—in truth, comic: comedy being my true nature; to understand this, my monsters must have ceased to astonish, and as yet, few are they who near that astonishment.

Instead of groups, monuments, and customs that have disappeared, a figure, several figures of service, in degraded settings, places more domestic, urban or rural; to accompany, heal, cheer my organism's own degradation and the progression of a hallucinatory sense, which grows more intense the more my body loses its flesh: ghosts of life surrounded by ghosts of my own.

In lieu of the constraints of cultural construction, relinquishing to the faery nature of humans, animals, diet, or plants; the passage of friendly figures, beloved, alive, their bodies transformed, settling progressively, in the text, into their true names.

*

The project, to record a fragment of *The Book*, proceeds and takes shape in August, in Paris. The intended producer, M.N., who financed my July 1975 investigation in Algiers, then in Tebessa, on the life and death of my friend Mohamed Laïd Moussa, takes us to lunch on a very high floor of the new hotel Nikko, along the Seine.

The luster of the place, the height of the backdrop, mirrors in abundance, multiple voices, convergent, divergent, opinions, schemes, the exaltation of some, the reserve of others, everything consumes me. Because I am all this at once: the lights, the voices, the beating hearts, the numbers, solidity, liquidity, abstraction, concreteness, fixity, movement.

I am only well when I am what is necessary to be the other.

What little I am becoming—and that little, ingested here—feeds my need—reason now leads my heart—to enter, above all else, into the self of he or she to whom speech is predominantly directed, perhaps touching a secret of his or her life, the dread, then, here and everywhere, that the other might be hurt, even minutely, pulls my soul, from soul at last, from pure will. From raw soul, life.

That late summer marks the end of my emotional self, the disappearance of all wounds of self-esteem, of all that builds the torment, the pleasure of so-called private life. The other, whomever he or she may be, becomes my sole concern.

I become the one to wound myself, I take on the reasons of that abruptness, injustice, jealousy and most of all, lack of faith—life's desolation: up to the very reasons of its lack of faith, fibrous laziness.

The recording takes place under the best conditions, in a studio on rue Montorgueil: during a month or two, several hours a day, the sound artist G.B. and I work over every word, letter, interval, and every breath of the chosen excerpt, thirty pages in which ancient Ethiopians appear, those whom Herodotus and Strabo call the Ethiopians of long life.

Through our mother's mother, my brothers, sisters, and I descend from a merchant peddler who, entering the country very young, in the retinue of a great nobleman from France, Italy or West Africa, perhaps even Egypt—where our maternal great-grandfather dies of cholera at the end of the nineteenth century—but with an Ethiopian name, "Tazana," gallicized into "Tézenas" in the first half of the sixteenth century, settles in Forez, at Boën-sur-Lignon, the Lignon of Honoré d'Urfé's *L'Astrée*, as a merchant draper, and marries his daughters to the nobles of that province, a principality at the time, himself ennobled, of the robe, at the end of his life.

That work, listening to the cut, in early autumn, of the text written in winter, and the effort of breath on very short pulmonary distance—an effort of musical interpretation—which the editing process seizes and cuts—sometimes, a letter, a second, an echo of a word, perhaps of a single letter, consonant or vowel, cut or drawn out—listening to my own breath, from that day or the previous, or from the week before, for connection or harmony, that return of my throat into my ear, an orphic reversal conducted hour after hour, by myself and by the man who will become a friend, that vocal, microscopic, technical decomposition, in a single, closed

place, of an act accomplished outside and through the operation of creative hallucination, leaves me exhausted, gaunt.

Machines with red, green, orange lights, portable micro-
phones on flexible stems like reptile mouths into which
I pour a kind of antidote, a taming liquid for the venom
of the world.

The sound of the tapes rolling, the gestures of the
technician interrupting the draw of the rotating disks;
working, sometimes, for almost thirty minutes on the
single pitch of a final consonant, on the fall of a breath,
an *f*, on the ending on a silent *e*. An entire activity of
suspension, a stay of life in the death of technique.

One evening, my friend invites me to dinner at his girlfriend's, near Versailles. In an apartment in a small
residential building, up in the trees: she, a perfume that
reminds me of bygone skin; children that are playing
upstairs. Forever inaccessible. Any household or dwelling
with mother-woman and children always appears to me
as the noblest of palaces.

Taken ill, in the middle of dinner, I regain consciousness
but they keep me for the night. I do not sleep, but I make
this night and these stars, near the open window, my
numerous Algerian nights spent on watch duty included,

myself so light, subject to pleasure—it is impossible to do anything without pleasure; and so I must adjust my duties, the demands of the profession, let them grow to the point of pleasure, and at that moment, act: that is the nature of my will, to cause such coincidence, to favor it, create it—into the most active contemplation of my adult life. The more I advance in life, the more the heavens are peopled with History: as if awaiting the arrival of a mythological chariot, or flying carpet, on which, the following season, I shall stage my whore Samora Machel and, leaving from Blida, have him cross the sea from Algiers to Marseille.

At breakfast, the silverware shines on the very red lips of the children; I already can't remember if I have eaten or not. In the bathroom, I caress the horn comb in which the mother's hair mingles with the curls of the children and several strands of the father's hair.

*

I spend time in the apartment of the concierge of the run-down building I have been living in for the past three years; we like each other a lot, she and I: she, still young, blond, and fresh. In her dark apartment, opening onto the courtyard and filled with small furniture, paintings, cloth, knickknacks of the kind you can still find in bazaars, small antique fountains with backlit waterspouts, she, very knowledgeable yet always in the midst of a lovers' breakup with its inevitable loss of money and household appliances, between two sobs as I soothe her, tells me, her shoulder bare, how much the sight of my room, lit up at night, for work, reassures her, and that I am among the night guardians of Paris.

The interior courtyard is often cluttered with objects to be returned to the previous lover, along with those of the new.

Every time, the large bed filling the recess at the back of the apartment is dressed with a new bedspread, heavy, embroidered, with tassels and pompoms.

Breakups and agreements are concluded, for the most part, harshly, over the phone: the device, resting atop a small dresser with a large three-dimensional pink rose, lit by the light of the roman fountain and a Burmese pagoda, is sheathed in tiger-skin velvet: in anger, her feet shed their golden mules, which are thrown over the fake leather ottomans toward the darker end of the room, under a fake piano of sorts, its keyboard lid sculpted into the wood—the foot of Samora angry at his pimp.

Sometimes, the deposed lover returns, or sends his henchmen threatening to recover goods: objects and situations confirm what I am configuring, upstairs, in my notebooks, covered in black paper.

# 7

In the middle of autumn, in southern Corsica, I meet my cousin J.-L., the son of my father's older sister, a prewar nurse on ocean liners, my godmother with whom, as a child, I write my first texts for a children's magazine she coedits, and who dies of bone cancer in 1952—her moans, her cries behind the padded door of the first-floor hallway and the closed shutters on the garden.

My cousin, raised in our hometown in the Rousseauist manner, barefoot in winter, very close to animals, has been working as a temp at the museum for many years. He captures small wild animals in West Africa and in Madagascar, bringing back, and leaving in my care, a lemur, a bat, and a magpie.

He lives near Porto-Vecchio with his charming family in a hut of sorts, without water or electricity, cultivating the fruit trees that grow around them, fishing for coral, and delivering bread in the early morning.

I set up my tent on a hillside and work face down, on the ground cloth, on the continuation of *Tales of Samora Machel.*

In the evening, when we're eating inside, his small pet, a civet—I imagine what its life was before captivity, as well as the life of its genitors—races about violently on the top shelves of the room.

Back in my tent, grasping Samora's body again, his eyes and ass, the folds between his shoulder and neck… I work, stomach against the ground, late into the night.

In the early morning, before 4 A.M., my cousin honks at the bottom of the hill and we leave for the mountains to fetch the bread—large loaves, baguettes, chocolate croissants—from the bakehouse, to distribute in the villages along the coast. We return at 8, my eyes are full of that blue and the sweep of the shore seen from above, I set to work again. I often don't have lunch. On the path leading to the house, I find a land turtle five to seven centimeters in length, Turtlette, which walks around my writing notebook and sometimes across it when I put off using it for too long.

In the late afternoon, I sometimes walk along the coast: on the way there and back, gunshots, and not from hunting. I work till nightfall, in the hollow of a smooth boulder, I imagine Samora's nocturnal transfers to Sardinia via the port of Saint Teresa, but it is much later, in 1980, in a Corsican sequence with Corsican words, that tough Sardinian smugglers and pimps will intervene.

For now, Samora's owner and manager is Algerian, the depressed and harmless Lahcene.

Two Riffian baker boys whom we speak to every morning warm their exhausted bodies outside: one of them, Manoudji...

Much later, because of their beauty and weariness, and the temporary servitude in which they find themselves, they shall be introduced into the vicinity of one of Samora's imaginary doubles, Noureddine... near the middle of the book, this time in the Goutte d'Or.

It does not immediately occur to me to transfer them into fiction: at the time, and even later, I do not feel the moral right to use figures—even more so when they are subjugated—a scene, information viewed or assimilated. Things must be forgotten for them to reappear in the natural flow of my imagination. Everything must pass through what constitutes my sole reality, my current, the flow, I do not want others to work for me. I cannot profit from misfortune or the spectacular nature of an event, yet perhaps imperceptibly, from day to day, and, especially, night to night, the figure does take shape, intimate details, the curve of a cheek, the nape of a neck, appear in other bodies as precursors of the figure *in full.*

I stay there a month and, on the mornings that follow, try to extract from my gaze anything that might appear to me as the budding curiosity of a realist author. I must first love those two exiles as they are, in their pure existence, irreplaceable and untouchable, without the filth of art; protect them even from the kind of nimbus of contempt they receive in the region, and from my own artistic gaze. And I see them only in the morning, in the vanishing darkness, until that time when they spread their half-naked, floured limbs upon the warm staircase.

\*

I meet the young son of a general—his house overlooks the sea—who hangs about with a languor of sorts and treats me gently. We walk together along the rocks among which the increased lightening of my weight allows me to maneuver. He knows my writing a bit and reassures me with a fragile certitude that I am not working in vain. He is one of those "untamed" readers, outside the scene, for whom the figures we have created are real figures and in sum, jumping from rock to rock in the crisscrossing of voices, these figures he speaks of are among us, even the most modest, the most fugitive, such as the little girl from

the First Song of *Tomb for 500,000 Soldiers*, or the little
sister in the dream of a soldier from the Fourth Song. The
blessing and terror of creating figures that shall be real to
the reader—and to the judge.

*

Day and night, when I write, the limit of what I write and
of the real world in which I do it is the coral, the live,
invisible enclosure of the island.

Coral is, in our colored nature, that which is without
apparent precious matter (sunsets are but gaseous,
ephemeral matter), a jewel, but we do not see that, it
lines the coast, a submarine ornament. Previously, in
Greater Kabylia, during the Algerian War, I imagined
that great territory barbed to the east, bordered by coral
to the north, embellished by much hope. And still now,
I place it upon the earrings of my whores, and have it
tinkle there.

So, in this late autumn, that color, which I do not see
but whose fishing and trafficking animates the coast over
which I write, is already watchful, alive, in the increased
darkening of my gaze. The resounding blue, a color I see
when returning from the bakehouse, becomes the color
of Antiquity, of *The Book*, of the perdition of History, of
the horror of being alone in it.

That red, submarine coral traces the inverted border of the fiction I am writing, its occult nature, the movements of its figures caught within the movements of the Great Desire—which is, for me, Life, which lies before me when I write, and which I tower over—at ease there, or constrained in their liquid bath... which is not the mother's local one, but... who can say it?... by a superior force that is the preexisting primordial rhythm (the rhythm that creates the world). My figures are born of my language, of that rhythm, in its bath.

One day at noon, we go to meet a woman in a village in the mountains. A member of her family has just been laid to rest there. The house is tall and cavernous. Women in black prepare lunch.

Upstairs, from the darkness, a scent I recognize: on the bed, an open silver casket, and, inside, gold, vermeil, pearl necklaces on the upturned lid; and from the bathroom, a smell of soap, of enamel that I recognize. Taken ill, not daring to stretch out on the bed, I lie on the floor instead. The scene of the night in which Samora rails against his depressed and negligent master, Lahcene, and starts a vengeful prophecy, with flying carpets, that scene—which I reconstruct and I continue, in the veering of the car, silently and simultaneously to the comments I make about the road, as well as in hellos, in kisses, and in stairways too—puts me to sleep or knocks me out. I fall asleep as I black out, blood in my mouth. Downstairs, they leave to bury the dead man or woman. In my intermittent moments of consciousness, the silence, the emptiness below, the absence of all those bodies stretched toward what it is suitable to be and do, seize me as I tremble. What have I done, or not done, that I am now so estranged from that centrifugal force of life: procreation. Of what have I not resisted poetry from the start?

But the *first* men, besides procreating, painted.

\*

Owls, fish, black pigs, coral in the beating water below.

To see the world as the water spider, the eagle, the mole—who sees so little—see it; to feel the world like the dust mite, the crab, or the whale; like the seagull in the cold settling on the crown of the king's statue, warming up there by defecating.

The eye is the organ that is least watery; to understand the world, one must love it, see it, feel it thus, with several eyes superimposed, several animal senses combined. The human eye would then be in addition; to think what animals think, man is no more the king of the universe than the lion is the king of animals. Man must also believe his evolution continues as the animal's evolution does. We must see ourselves as animals see us. Ever since I have discovered it, I have felt the evolutionist vision to be more grandiose than the vision of Creation, its historical space is immense, such an increase of time and space cannot damage the history of man and the beauty of his advent.

Painting: when I am in this frame of mind, which I believe to be the most beautiful, the most *moral*, to which those who profess to think should conform, nothing, even beauty itself, escapes reduction. Pain—is that not the goal of Art? What seems most universal, most indubitable to my human eye is challenged by other, animal gazes, in their size, their depth and height, or speed. Until the subway cricket, which also sings, teaches me that the most beautiful human music is the most beautiful of all music, I shall be unable to *believe* it.

My human senses, with their neuro-cervical organization, are what allow me to see and feel the absolute. With that systematic doubt, that instantaneous relativity of all the absolutes that compose us, I create one for myself, an absolute, and just as strong—yet fraught with more fatality. My search for the absolute leads to this: that I always desire more absolute still. All the absolutes created by man to which I have professed, I deprived them of their value as absolutes in regard to others that we, as yet, ignore. Such is perhaps absolute transcendence. "God" would have created all worlds, not simply the one wherein humanity stirs and begins to shift: humanity would be nothing but one of those tribes, a moment or parcel of life, but one that demands, with the strength of desperation, to have been alone created by Him. What I feel only sheds doubt on human absolutes, and cannot shed doubt on "God's" existence. Neither do I consider that man must adore Him (as they attempted to convince me as a child, in vain), nor that science annuls Him—from where, from simple human existence! We cannot reason on that existence, with fixity, time, and space: species evolving, others perhaps to come, space in expansion, with what speed can we think "God" or non-"God"?

"God" cannot have created the world with human senses: creating a species of insects, of fish, for example, wouldn't He watch the world through the eyes of the species He is creating? Isn't evolution the trajectory of God's thought, as he thinks creation to come and thinks it as a synthesis of His visions? The trajectory of Evolution = the trajectory of the thought of God the Creator.

There is something of this in human creation, in fiction, in how a figure appears and is formed. The temporality of the book is the temporality of evolution. What is ideal theater but the moment when the creator disappears in favor of his creature, when those creatures speak, answer one another beyond his control. When I think of such a scene, I hear the most beautiful language of desire.

What is desire?

Man conceives of "God" in space when he must think of him in time. Religious faith has reduced "God" to human limits. The religions of the Book and atheism reduce "God" to mere human limits.

If we only consider the human, the Gospel is really the accomplishment of the human heart. Yet if we withdraw from the human, with human senses and human reasoning, we can only feel a lack when we reread it today: all that is not human is not there, except a God, father and son, too human…

Often what saddens me the most is that the Christian heart has thought of nothing except the human. There is, of course, a human task to be accomplished with human means, but paradoxically, as all religions teach us, this is not enough for man, God's *internal* image…

From such lack, I do not arrive at the rhetorical complaint of our diminution and minuteness in the infinite…

Man has his voice in the chorus of the Universe, a voice no doubt equal to that of *others*, as in a beautiful system of democracy. Man is neither small, nor miserable, he is part of what, for a large part, for an endless part, remains unknown to us.

# FRUCTUS BELLI

mes et perdus ,            Monstrent bien que le crime (horrible et noire engeance)   Et que c'est le Destin des hommes vicieux
ux a cet arbre pendus     Est luy mesme instrument de honte et de vengeance ,       D'esprouuer tost ou tard la iustice des

inv. et sc.

## 8

One of my mother's sisters, Clothilde, is dying at the Broussais Hospital (red brick buildings with high slate roofs, today gone), in the 14th Arrondissement.

Very beautiful—our mother often praises her thick, brown locks to us children—born in Poland like all her brothers and sisters. At the end of the Resistance, after what she has lived through and witnessed in the Fresnes Prison, she decides, in August 1944, amid the incomprehension of most of those closest to her, to break her engagement with a young, handsome and rich Argentine descendant of the family of German poet Adelbert von Chamisso, the *Man Who Lost His Shadow*, and hailing from the Champagne region, and to enter (taking a vow of poverty, and chastity) the Mission de France.

A certified nurse, used to prewar balls and outings, she now works as a ward orderly in the Paris hospitals, then in Algiers, then again in Paris, and, finally, in Lyon, closest to the humble of this world. Sometimes she comes to visit us and our mother: what I perceive of the conversation between the two sisters confirms for me, a child still, that I am, in myself, closer to her absolute commitment than to the one my mother confronts her with—against her own wishes.

She immediately gives away everything that is given her. Dispossession of all that is not the self, then dispossession of the self.

As the years go by, even her language changes, simplifies, even shatters between the language of her origins and the one she hears at work, yet the passionate flow of her brothers and sisters' speech, of our mother's, to a lesser degree, is maintained: as I am then beginning to refuse the codes used by part of the class to which I belong, to suffer from the rules and the regulation that reduce its passion, destroy its soul, her language is sanctity—that is how I see that commitment then and how I see it now: the "smell of sanctity" is language above all, the voice of the saint, a voice that tears off its bandages.

In Algiers, in Paris, then in Lyon, at the risk of her life and honor, she hides wanted Algerian militants and prostitutes pursued by their pimps, in the slums of Givors.

As I am committed to the creation, the accompaniment, the transformation, and the transference of heat unto my figures, how could I not help her die, she who had given herself over to others: and thus compensate for her lack of understanding of what I write, what I do…

I make a habit of visiting her bedside and staying there till midnight.

Every night, around 8 P.M., I break off my couplings, go out, walk toward the hospital.

During my time as a soldier in Algeria, she alone regularly worries about me. I receive a weekly letter from her with a selection of newspapers. During my interrogation in early spring 1962, the colonel of the Second Bureau of Military Security prides himself in having had his boots shined by Krim Belkacem, who is his subordinate before going underground and later participating in the launch of the Algerian Insurrection in November 1954. He goes so far as to read, boots on table, from my confiscated papers, some of the letters in which she agonizes over the fate of the young conscripts with a passion that makes him laugh. That day, as I experience a lapse, a doubt as to whether my commitment to Independence is just, as do all prisoners of opinion, his mockery rouses me, all the revolt and sacrifices endured under Nazism by the sisters and brothers of our mother, of our father, by she whom he now taunts, rises in my throat, hardens my joints: I hurl them at him violently. Just as I have been since my days in boot camp in Grenoble, I am described as being prone to anger to the point of blows yet subject to cardiac erethism, the socialite of the Circle stops short.

She begins her death now, out of exhaustion rather than sickness, I straighten her pillows, her hair, *longhaired Samora*, help her drink—what absolute is she still thirsting for? She has always loved me as she does my sisters and brothers, although my writing and some of my political and social activities at the time—soldier's defense committees, Lyon prostitutes, etc.—upsets her.

As one of my sisters does, caring for my mother in her final months—my mother, who wishes in her later years to distribute her love equally between her children, and so deprives my sister of the excess affection she usually bestows—I attend to and prepare her beauty, for her final moment, for her deliverance unto the beyond—but what remains of her faith, then?

My mother, as she nears death, before she lets her sons into her bedroom, and this until the morning of her dying day in which we all take part, is and allows herself to be made prettier by our sisters.

She dies one night after my visit. Because she has bequeathed her body to Science, and, as she is our mother's sister, I struggle to leave the room in the morgue where I have helped to place her body in the drawer, I have set a small bouquet in her hands and left a note for the "carvers."

Her burial: I withdraw from the comedy, I remain in our common exception.

This time I spend between the obscurity of zones of sexual congress and the word of *Tales of Samora Machel*—candles, kerosene lamps, breaths—and the night vigil in the hospital room where our mother's sister breathes with the same breath as she.

# 9

January 1st, 1980, a friend drives me, without my mobile residence but with my work, to a large house in the countryside around Aix-en-Provence, a small wing of which he uses to house himself, his girlfriend, and his painting studio, near the place where Sam Francis lives and paints in the early 1950s, whom I shall later meet to work with him on a book, *Wanted Female*.

I settle at the other end of the vast house overlooking the Eguilles Valley, in a large sitting room with china in cabinets and small furniture that belonged to late Enlightenment libertines. My bed is made of two sofas, face to face, on which I sleep as if in a golden conch. The porcelain echoes.

A round pedestal table, a worktable. Right away, I set the black notebooks of *Tales of Samora Machel* upon it.

The room, whose furniture and objects I uncover, opens directly onto the top of the park (it faces the orangery) where in previous years I had parked my work van, with its external annex, the deckchair-tablet with parasol, to write *The Book*.

Winter is cold and luminous. I am anxious to resume the work I interrupt the night before. When I breathe, I feel my blood. Everything chimes in this space, even the night, birds bewildered by the frost strike against the south side shutters that I am told to keep closed. The following day, we go to Camargue. To Montmajour. Despite the great cold, near Port-Saint-Louis, I decide to swim, I enter the tempestuous sea; back at the car, my right hand gets stuck in the door, I shall have three fingers bandaged for the next six months.

In February, I can go outside to work on a high garden table, round, green, its top very small, with just enough room for the notebook, my right wrist and my left hand holding the pages down against the wind. Behind me, the wall and windows of the orangery to the south. My friend's two beautiful children, with their father, rally around my work and the very despair that supports and accentuates it. The eldest, five years earlier, works with leather, and sells his goods near Saint-Guilhem-le-Désert.

With his blond beauty, the charm of his speech, his art of bargaining, he sells within hours what he has produced in a week. He makes me a white leather satchel the size of a large wallet that I can strap to the bottom of my leg above my foot.

He is now 17, his satchel would no longer stay up on my leg, which has already grown very thin, it would slide onto the ankle and I would walk on it. The youngest child draws and paints with his father at the other end of the southern side of the house, facing the great trees. If it were not incumbent upon me to carry my figures to their temporary term, and to continue loving what in the world is not loved, I would wish to be reduced to a pot, without earth nor flowers, reduced to the blade of a spade: even as a child I stare at inanimate, "insentient" objects and envy their state: rocks, motor parts, even words, abstract ones, especially from philosophy.

Although before me lies the most industrious and luminous plain, and beyond, the sea most charged with myth, my sole reality is the page on which I write, endowed with more reality than the world, objects, closed or exterior spaces, the light in which I make my figures move.

My love, however, draws me to the humblest of objects: scrap, school notebooks in public dumps, the gaze of children, the dribble of idiots, those are what can be looked at in full; art objects, antiques, the gaze of adults, books, monuments, harvests, all of that constitutes a reality for others. Text aside, what elevated discourse I take on, be it reasoning, the expression of learning, is as if spoken by someone other than me, speaking, explaining, persuading, even. My distress is already inexpressible; I want it undetectable by others in my voice.

When, at dinner, a well-known musician, A.B., who is temporarily renting a room in the house, asks me for subjects of opera librettos, I provide the one about the life and disappearance of Louis XVII. I have it from my mother, who, herself, learned it from her father, whom the Naundorff mystery interested to such a degree that, when he travelled from Poland to France in the interwar period, he visited those cities where the most famous of pretenders lived, to gather information from their archives…

What other subject can I provide than one so related to my writing: through subverted morality—inverted hierarchy, debauched innocence, scorned maternity: disappearance of the human into the non-human, continuous sexual use.

I imply that at the core of the project lies the transformation of the language, the voice of the young Dauphin, then of the young king (scene of his proclamation as king and of his mother kneeling at the Temple upon hearing of his father's decapitation), into the language and the voice of the people. A kind of intoned metaphor of the tragedy issuing from within myself, inside my art, inside myself, issuing from the transformation of my writing into language—before, later, after coma, into Word.

Among the few extant accounts of how that defamilialized, deposed, and degraded child speaks, of his few violent phrases ("When are those whores to be clipped!"), of his cocky, cobbler's apprentice way of speaking, of the freeing of his sexual instinct, I could cull enough to charge with flesh, with vocal flesh, and to shake up the opera scene at the time...

My idea, understood, is rather quickly deferred. Despite the beauty of his music, A.B. fears my subject and the word he knows I would bring into play.

In mid-February, a doctor makes me take a new treatment. My improvement, which owes much to the tenderness of my friends, ceases at once. The work at hand fills with doubles, with the ghosts of humans, whores, animals, as if I needed to reinforce, to prolong the tenderness of earthly exchanges in the life of those who embrace in their beyond.

# 10

On March 9, I interrupt *Tales of Samora Machel* with the death of one his companions from the "Village Nègre." An acquaintance of ours, a very strong boy, motherless since birth—his father is a great military doctor who treated Houari Boumediene at the end of his life—and who is a talented apprentice architect-archeologist, specialist of Ancient Rome and endowed with a pro-Roman radicality that his physical strength increases tenfold and renders threatening, suggests a trip from Roman forums that are known to Roman forums yet to be discovered, all the way down to southern Italy.

We leave the following afternoon in an uncertain Citroën 2cv that we will use as living space, along with my Corsican tent. At night, in the streets of Genoa, I am

40 years old since January, an age that, as an adolescent, I had decided not to live beyond. The renewed joy of driving ceases abruptly. Optical illusions take over once again, the facades of patrician houses and palaces appear in their tripled power; perspectives are increased two, threefold because of everything I know of what preceded them in History. So many individual, collective lives from which I am shut out. I feel this separation even more as I, since childhood, cannot get used to the fact that it is impossible to embrace, in one human life, each of the billions and millions of human lives, those ongoing and those in the process of being born, as I cannot see an illuminated window without feeling the regret, the rage of not being among those living there—and wolfing down the soup. In addition to which the billions of billions of billions of so-called animal lives to be lived, died, "birthed" then…

We drive through the upper city looking for a fountain next to which we can stop and sleep. My first night out of the china sitting room pulses with the irregular tossing of my companion's muscle mass upon the two upturned seats; the cold, the restlessness of animals running beneath the car cannot distract me from an anxiety that shall remain contained till the end of the trip, stretched taut within me, inside this body that I shall strive to keep limber, even slightly neglected. But who, outside myself, save for R., my beloved brother, and a few others who are very close, knows of my internal battle and its manifestations, minute or even invisible to "others"?

In the very early morning, washing up at the fountain: children, women, workers, already walking to their work, the hope, between obscurity and sunlight, that the torment shall be eluded, that day…

In Carrara in the afternoon, at the foot of the site, the resounding vision of artisans crafting Antique and Renaissance replicas of impure marble, the ease of their work, its familial structure, wife at the cash register, children screaming in the playgrounds near the schools, disorients me: happiness is there, inaccessible, in the modest act of duplication, learnt from a school master or on the job, and transmitted to future husbands and fathers… oh… heavens!

Instead of which, the movements, the screeches of cables and pulleys we perceive, the cries, the worker's songs, in the mountain above, within the marble crags, are the sounds of my athletic work of the year before, reconstitutions, from within, of ancient scenes, Greek, Roman, Persian, Indian, Judean, Philistine…

I cut my bread and other things with my friend Agnes' small fish-shaped knife. She has big, curly black hair, small, very hard breasts, and her nudity always seems to be emerging from under brambles or water—a friend and I see her, that last summer, in Paris, her tender head sticking out from under the white sheet of an intensive care unit.

On the Carsulae plateau, north of Terni, in the early morning, after a night in the vehicle near Acquasparta and a long dream (a tunnel through which I am chased, naked, by dogs—something at least tangible in my life), we find ourselves in the ruins of the city of shining stones, the crevices still full of snow. It was long ago a military out-post of Vespasian, the first destructive Roman besieger of Jerusalem and enemy of Vitellius, he for whom the body of an enemy always smells good. Weakened because the Via Flaminia is deviated toward the east, the city, at the time, houses what remains, head and knees, of a giant statue of Emperor Claudius, born in Vienne on the Rhône, at the foot of the mountain where I was born, and where Pontius Pilate, named proconsul after his term in Judea, is said to have hurled himself into the Rhône out of remorse.

Passing beneath the arc of Saint Damian, I see that small painting from the Louvre, of the decapitation of Saint Cosmas, Saint Damian, and others, their bodies spewing blood and heads haloed in gold on the ground. I no longer want Art at that point, but decapitation, yes! and with Agnes' knife all I can do is cut my throat...

After one of the following nights spent in the car, in the snow in Abruzzo with all fountains frozen, still in the dark, we enter a bakery to buy freshly baked bread. The family invites us in, offers us a bath and coffee with milk, and until midafternoon, when the father returns to work, we remain in the small back room, speaking a mix of Italian and French, discussing what they believe is plaguing Italy, the Red Brigades, corruption, the lack of a strong state. They are close to tears as they speak.

Why am I not the child, the girl rather, so as to lose my self more surely in the other gender, who, in the back room, hums her lessons at the table?

In the Manfredonia Gulf, at the back of the Saint Michael Archangel Sanctuary, in the middle of the white village, beneath the Norman castle of Giants, above the sea, during Holy Week, the ex-votos.

On the heights overlooking the coast, we spend two nights in an international excavation site, on camp bunks under a tent: in the morning of the first night, as I am slow to rise—the body's ascension—my comrade throws his shoes at my head. At morning's end, we are on a coast of flat stones, entering a white seaport village at the top of a large street leading to the sea: silence, not a living soul except for a dog; from one side of the line of parallel white buildings to the other, a black rope is stretched and tied in the middle around the throat of a puppet made of cloth, wood, and cardboard, a brown-haired prostitute with a red dress and a black purse. On the rope and along each side of the puppet, a strip of white paper flapping in the wind, on which the words "*E morta come ha vissuto*" are written, an inscription as might seem reserved for the figures of all my writing, past, current, and future.

The evening of Holy Thursday, we climb up to a large village that is celebrating the Crucifixion, in the night.

On the vast plaza along the nave of the church, trestle tables are set up, on these trestles three high crosses, on the center one, the highest, the body of a young man, scrawny, wiry—passing vagrant or mental patient or freed prisoner?—is standing, loincloth around his thighs, arms on the arms of the cross; on each side of him, two fleshy youths—the life of pleasure of the thieves—hold similar positions; coming from a loud-speaker perched in a high illuminated window of the presbytery where we see the head and trembling hands of the priest, the *Ride of the Valkyries*. From the butcher shop across the street come cuirassed, short-skirted centurions; from the bakery and the notions store, veiled and bowing, the Holy Women.

The children are sitting near the trestles, the moonlight alone would be enough to illuminate this performance of the Tragedy that is recited in the intervals of the music, alternately in Italian and in Latin, by the priest into his microphone.

At the end of the Crucifixion, the mothers recover their thievish sons and Christ is brought down, shaking with the tremors of cold, placed, beyond the trestles, on a stretcher carried by counselors and municipal employees preceded and followed by a crowd of Christian Democrat children playing the fife; to the cemetery where a rapid burial and instantaneous retrieval of the body takes place.

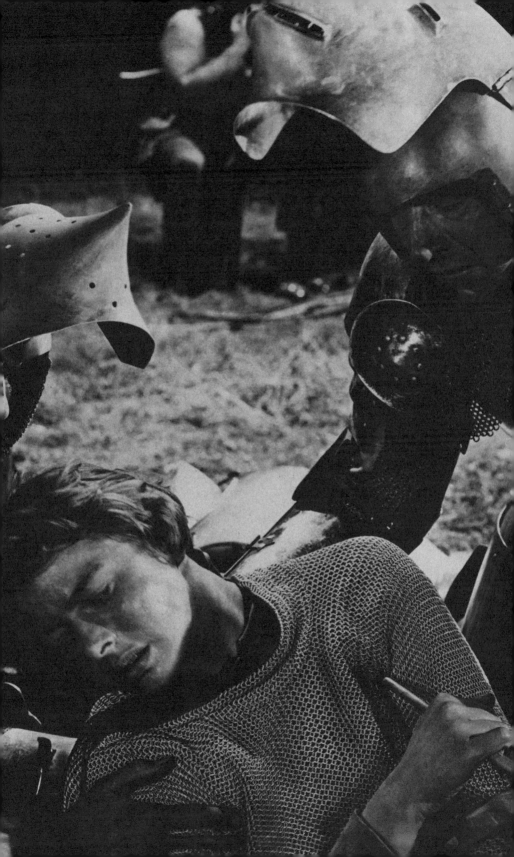

11

Back in France, I return to Broussais for several days of observation and check-up. In addition to the usual exams, a young psychiatrist from the medical ward visits me—who has him come to my room?—and with a voice too soft and too firm, presses his school principles into my body and soul in suspension.

The only thing I could be cured of is no longer writing, but I never complain of the rest. What joy of living I possess resides entirely in that tension and back-and-forth, that interior game between an illness I have known since childhood to afflict all humans at once, namely to be nothing but that, human in a mineral, vegetable, animal, divine world, and a recovery that no one would desire, that would deprive me, if it were to succeed, of all courage, all desire, all the pleasure of pushing ever beyond, ever onward—and which, having long known where my interests lie, I do not want.

He also asks me what I "do": I intimate that I write and regret my confession immediately, as he is among those who attempt to reduce their patients under the pretext of an equalizing sickness; as I later learn, in a diner in town that very evening, and against all morality, he mentions that morning's encounter, his doubts about my identity: "I saw someone who claims to be a writer and whose name is apparently...," the guests, who know my fictions and their fame at the time, rebut him, and envy his being able to see me, to speak to me, if not touch me.

A short while after this observation period, I check into the Saint-Michel Hospital, the archangel of soldiers, for a varicose vein operation on both legs.

*Stripping*, an American method that is just then being introduced in France, is the deveining, stripping of veins, their isolation with a knife: the veins are pulled, cut, shortened.

I am in a room with twelve beds, six facing another six.

The day before the general anesthesia, an intern casually, clumsily, draws the incisions on the back of my legs with a violet marker. That tattoo over the top of what shall be scratched out from the inside between muscles and nerves, although it reminds me of the reality of writing, reinforces the humiliation in which I live without living, yet without which one cannot dare think, where is the greatest truth, where is the greatest beauty, in the words that follow them on the surface like detectors, or in the depths of our inner life, our inner art?

Despite my cheer—pain or pre-pain always provokes euphoria of word and empathy in me—to be marked in this way, even on my legs, caught between the advanced age of the eleven patients and the tiled, dilapidated obscurity of the place in which I see and sense spaces of the past as well: middle-school infirmaries, hospice wood paneling, my beginnings in the human community as it were, I experience—but from which "I" then?—and keep from my family and friends, a sensation the operation should resolve, of inexistence between two kinds of senescence, of dispossession, failure, abandonment by Light, cold humiliation, oblivion. I am just emerging, however, from the light and wealth of what I write during the previous season—and from the false, inaccessible light of my travels in Italy, which conceals and crushes it.

Contrasts have never frightened me (they are even a proof of sorts that I am finally living a "real" adult life), yet here, for the first time perhaps, I no longer see a future for myself, and no longer see myself in the future of others.

Perhaps the practitioners have decided upon this operation only to distract me from what they do not understand and cannot soothe: depression; in other words, a physical intervention to defer their encounter with the intangible?

In the same movement, they also do a poor operation on frenulum breve of the penis. To distract me from my core affliction; and entertain themselves there.

After the operation, and a very difficult awakening, I am terrorized when my eyes encounter the same immobility, when my nostrils and ears perceive the fetid smell and moans of the old men in the room—at that moment, I lose track of my age, 40, which as a child I had decided never to live beyond—back from double, triple coronary bypasses.

But on my left, two beds from mine, near the closed end of the Large Hall, a man awakens from the amputation of his right leg because of gangrene: every night he will weep, will scream for his missing leg.

He makes an effort to limit the volume of his shouts and cries, speaks to his phantom leg, touches its calf, pulls its hair, scratches its ankle, stretches and kneads its toes, bangs its knee. His leg—where is it now? thrown away? burned? chopped, mixed into dog food?—itches. It shakes when he dreams, when, very rarely, he dreams, he dreams himself whole.

Maître d'—why gangrene?—in a somewhat luxurious Parisian restaurant, he talks to us—forgetting, as he speaks, his missing leg—about his work, his good luck. In the same way, ages ago, for two years in a row, in the barrack rooms, guardrooms, watchtowers, toilets in mountain-peak posts and construction sites, some of my comrades from Algeria—bellhops, waiters, doormen in civilian life—narrate with putrid crudity their exploits with beautiful and rich women, always American, always older.

At night I see him, touching the toes of his raised, missing leg. As he has been suffering for the past several months at home and then here, the toenails are grown and bent, he cuts them on his left leg, he also cuts them on his missing right leg. Anxiety muffles his plea: will he be able to continue the job he loves, one day, with a wooden leg or an artificial limb?

My own legs wrapped in bandages, I go down to the garden—the clinic, today abandoned or destroyed, is being renovated: machines gnaw away at a bit more of the greenery every day.

The gardener, an Algerian of my age, but sturdier, imposing even, a gentle face, abundant black curls, the gaze and manner of a child still, shows me his leg where veins ripple, large and blue, especially in the fold behind the knee: in our conversation, place-names from Eastern Algeria come up: douars, hamlets, mountain passes, forests, shrines, springs, cascades, bridges, gorges, crossroads.

His young daughter brings him lunch, which he eats in the back of the garden: one stormy afternoon, she carries away the plate and silverware from her father's meal wrapped in a white cloth; legs bound, heavy, in bandages, I cross the front desk of the hospital with her, and, in a neighboring street, follow her up into the apartment of a family of friends: young girls strap heavy and multicolored school bags onto their shoulders; she washes the plate and silverware in the sink; hands in the dish towel, facing me, she asks me to tighten the pink ribbon in her very black hair; and turns and bends her head; I untie the ribbon, stretch the hair on her nape, grab it to tie the ribbon; tighten the knot; move back to an armchair where I sit and watch that nape—for me, the most poignant place on the body along with the fold of the groin—moving in the slightly fatty obscurity of the sink; from the great blue sky—or from a latrine on the same floor, or an uncovered pâté?—a fly alights—as long ago, one, then two, three, on my mother's face, finally delivered of her agony. I must go back; I move up to the young girl who hasn't stirred—she, accustomed for generations to the flies of livestock and misery; and, my eye on the contour of her cheek, staring at the edge of the batting eyelashes, kiss that bent nape from where the fly darts.

# 12


Leaving the clinic, all I want is to go home and tend to my own convalescence, but faced with what my friends and family might feel to be agitation, I am compelled to check into the psychiatric ward at Saint-Antoine. I do not stay long, there is nothing to treat (but always and again the humiliation of being a subject, a brain being judged: what a horrible experience that is for a creator).

Staying with my youngest brother, in the middle of Nature, in the Beaujolais, near his children, especially his young daughter, I try to strengthen what resolutions my improved physiological state can now withstand, but which my weakened, vanished desire to live cannot take on.

The presence, in the shed, of my live-in vehicle, whose wheels I have replaced, the dwelling place of some my most rebellious and sweetest sounding writing, momentarily arrests the question of the future.

I follow my brother along on his routes, on the other side of the Saône and on the other side of the Rhône rivers; in La Côte-Saint-André, we have lunch near the so-called Pavilion of the Curse, where Doctor Berlioz, father of Hector, is said to have doomed his rebellious son to failure.

I endeavor to relocate what little interior current I still possess into the collective current of the human community; I even wish for that frail current to be swept away there. Living without others is impossible, yet if you give yourself up to them, you disappear in them. And thus I have disappeared into my fictive figures, into the Italian ones, into those closest to me, and who draw from me what they dare not draw from God himself. Since my childhood, I see movement in humanity, rather than fixed turpitude, I see the struggle that each being wages to live. Who can see the struggle that the little I might become wages to save that little in advance?

Nearer to the Rhône, we pass within view of our mother's home which is to be sold before the year's end; higher up, on a plateau of ponds (where we swim as children and which I paint at the time, sitting on the sluice floodgate), alongside a large residence where, as a small child at the end of the war, I discover, in a high room, a little girl in pink, reading and writing at a desk: with her left hand, because her right arm is missing.

The very next day I want to return to that house, several kilometers away from ours, and continue to read with the little girl, I see her again, but outside, near the pools, between the mythological statues.

\*

Further down, the road closes off the Artas valley, where, as a child, at the close of a summer following the war—is it the first time, since war is declared, that we stay in our family home, on the other side of the Rhône, at the time under Italian fascist rule?—our mother takes me, alone, one very hot, dusty afternoon, air motionless, to this glen we climb halfway, where great white cows recline beneath willows with no birds, on a ground of bare clayey earth; slightly down the slope, a bathtubtrough of stagnant water rests, around which young dogs frolic on a bed of hay.

A bull (hair bristled) butts his curled brow against the enclosure of his corral.

Upright on a fallen tree trunk, our mother reads *The Lily of the Valley*; the sound of the turning pages joins the rasp and drone of insects, the yapping of the dogs in the straw, the rumination of the cows and the noise of tails slapping against their rumps.

A dog, older, emerges from beneath the fence of the corral: the other dogs have lifted a dry red-streaked bone from the straw and fight over it: dropping the bone, they run toward the older dog, surround him and push him toward the straw bed, knocking him over, his back onto the bone: the dog, upside down, legs in the air, has teats like a cow; our mother closes the book, smiles at me and daydreams.

A bellow of the bull scatters them all; and now the young dogs return, one by one, onto the straw I have drawn near: the dogs, suddenly, surround me, lick me and knock me down, weigh down upon me, yet their sunny disposition, the silky coolness of their bodies makes me shiver, their lapping in my folds, along the joints of my body... an eyes closes in upon mine, my vision shrinks, bordered by black while my heart...

Waking, one of them braces himself against the small of my back, as I bend down to lift myself from the group: the bull rebellows, the dogs rescatter.

*

A friend, X., comes to get me, as if to save me from my terror of Nature, bring me back to the city: at that point, I am with the children on a road between a stream and a long charred ruin, whose story I invent for them.

In the city, Lyon, I resume with nightlife: the exceptional cosmic situation which night constitutes for ordinary man always carries with it the hope, if not that a new me is to be established within, at least that I find some respite within the one that afflicts me. To refound the self in the place, the time and the state of the human, in the full light of day, and with others around living fully in that light, is perhaps natural for humans attuned, but is a vain task for those who have ceased to be. At night, in the hemisphere, the greater part of work and society in sus-pension—the other hemisphere, laden with noise, with light, with smells, lies at such a remove from my feeble body that I feel how inefficient it is to recover what I have lost—during the hiatus of the world, *I* can think it natural that *I* stop as well—and yet, I do not sleep.

Later, my brother R., with whom I spend time in Lyon, takes me to Saint-Jean-de-Bournay, to what remains of our summerhouse, sold to a childhood friend of our uncle who was deported and missing in Germany. We can still sleep there, I stay in what we call "the church book bedroom," which belonged, during her adolescence, to my mother's sister who died last winter in Broussais.

On the wall to the right of the bed, a beautiful period copy, in a golden frame, of the *Turkish Bath* by Alexandre-Gabriel Decamps.

The next day, I, who have always felt guilty sleeping, for whom sleeping is made for dreaming and dreaming for being—not being?—and living otherwise, for whom sleeping during the day is terrifying because each time I sleep, it is as if I were dying, and upon waking had to be reborn, I cannot leave that metal bed, I can't fall asleep, I did not sleep, I search in the Decamps, in what still remains of the day, in my heart even, for reasons to rise. It is 5 in the afternoon, my brother comes to me, bends over and helps me, sad as well; it is the same situation, this time reversed, as the one, long ago at dawn, in the small mountain school, when the priest on watch in the one-room dormitory of forty beds, leaving his alcove, very gently reorients me, with words, back toward my bed; I, a sleepwalker, already poised to go out into the pasture.

My brother travels with me, in my van, toward Martigues where I will settle near some friends. We pass through Vienne, along the Gervonde River and its bankrupt industries, textiles, tanneries, a few feet away from the

Roman ruins, theater, temple, which, as a child, I can't wait to see again, come summer.

But on the other side of the Gervonde River, which runs through and separates the northeastern part of town from the rest, a vast and high neighborhood of slums steeps in the waters soiled by the waste from high-end textiles factories. Facades, wood or cob overhangs loom above the river.

The Gervonde springs from a pond, to the east of Vienne, where we go swimming. The river, winding between orchards and vegetable gardens on a small plateau, runs alongside the road, then, encased in a canal level with the road—as children we play at running as fast as the current or running upstream as fast as it goes down (we throw a floating object into it)—leads, at the end of the plateau, to a washhouse where women, wearing flowered dresses and their hair down, beat the laundry daily, with cradles, baby carriages and strollers lined up beneath the awning.

The river then flows down a small waterfall onto the plain, running behind a milk factory, the smell of which wafts up the small geological rift toward the washhouse where the women bend their breasts, at times bared at night, when, in the dimming light, the insects multiply above the water. As a child, I think that the milk processed in the factory below is the one that comes out of the breasts above.

I sense something of an industrial link, an economic current between these washhouse women and the factory milk; I know that the milk we are supposed to drink comes from the cows I often see being milked in the farms at night. But seeing the milk cans filled with cow's milk, in the mountain, along the roads, at crossroads, often against a wayside cross, or a Missionary or rechristianizing cross made of stone or cast iron with a stone base, and knowing that those white tin cans, small and large, are collected in trucks and their contents distributed to the creameries, and the grocery stores, I later grow accustomed to reality: the milk processed by the factory is cow's milk.

The river enters the town, runs in a canal alongside the street where the foundations of our residence take root, and then set free from the canal, crosses the Détourbe plain to Vienne and the Rhône with its current, which is freed at that point, and violent most of the time...

Laundry hangs from the windows of the slums, hordes of kids run and scream in the alleyways...

How do you clean up a hovel? How do you clean what is dirty, soiled from the inside: the wood, the floors, the stairway steps, the toilets on the landing, the walls, the cob impregnated to the bone by two or three centuries of... cooking, laundry, the saliva of love, the spittle of anger, the snot of children, vomit, feces, bad weather, cats, and industrial smoke?

In middle school, every week, for our Saint Vincent de Paul Conference, we visit and help the indigent, wash their dwellings and bring them food; an old man, working class, widower, who lives on the mezzanine floor of a hovel in downtown Saint-Chamond, sitting on his straw chair, shows us, makes us smell the toilet main of his building that passes through his wall, then beneath his tiled floor, and in bad weather, oozes.

\*

In Martigues, on the southern side of the Étang de Berre: between my friends' house and the rock outcrop, I once again settle with my van for the night and the whole season. In the house: stereo system always keeping vigil on the world, family mess—clean laundry to iron, toys to put away. The path of foodstuff, objects, swimming, sporting gear, bath toys, and school clothes thickens until it reaches the domain of childhood, the two boys' two rooms with two "beds," rendering it nearly inaccessible. Firm yet quasi-invisible reign of the adults over the children, movement of the adult voices in those of the children and of the childish voices in the adult ones, appearance and abundance of family meals, tenderness in my brother's distant explanations about my state.

I stay awake at night hoping that if I sleep in the vehicle in which I work and travel in the desert, after all those months of insomnia in grounded places, I shall be delivered.

Insomnia, and the pressure of light on the window panes, on my heart, runs a stake through my chest, and leaves me taut, in the early morning, upon the bunk from which I spring, formerly, desert, plateaus, torrents, Roman ruins, forests, town centers, with such joy for the day of work or travel ahead, alone or against others…

My brother leaves us at noon, how is it possible that he is in life and I am not? How, born of the same mother, can we be separated so?

The following evening, before dinner, at night, my friend comes to the van, we walk a while beneath the pines—the pine is the tree of sex, of Antiquity, in its trunk it garners the profusion of life and its shadow burns, consumes, it is the tree of inaccessible joy: how can one *be* two thousand years ago, now, and two thousand years hence, at the same time?

Anxiety has me shaking from head to toe, my friend clasps me to him, his words are what my entire body awaits: I am in the world.

# 13

Early the next morning, outside, between my van and the rocks, I resume work on my large red writing case that is hinged to a lounge chair. I want to write a beginning for *Tales of Samora Machel*, which I have taken in stride again since July 1979: it shall be another of the "re-beginnings" of this as yet unpublished text. I have enough technical and artistic strength to write the entry and exit for any book, whatever it may be. But here, for *Tales of Samora Machel*, the question again emerges of the right that we do or do not possess, creators of figures that we are, to decide that one of our figures will *appear*, or worse, the "central" figure—before that other right, of equal importance, to decide that it will disappear or die.

Painting guides my hand: my entire future creation is in my interior gaze: when the torments of my life cease, it comes to lie before me: the figures of what future fictions I shall write are there, all of them before me with all of their backing, their settings, their lighting, their depth like a painting of Creation, it is up to me to animate them now, to have them speak without lifting an eye from them. But how can I make them speak from my mute throat?

And, haunted as I am by History, by Prehistory, by Evolution, not only for the human, but also for the animal, the vegetable, the mineral, the object, how can I resolve to make a figure appear for the sole reason of action or of "art"? I must have superior reasons, a more distant logic, so that the figures emerge from my "breast" at least, just as they do for the Creator, so that they surface from what I sense of my infinitude.

Thus, they rise from that rhythm-mass, and must remain linked to it, undifferentiated momentum and result.

*

End of summer, beginning of autumn, I write more than a hundred pages of a new beginning for *Tales of Samora Machel*: the scene is Polynesia and they speak Tahitian with its *i, a, u, ow* and its glottal pause so near to Arabic pronunciation.

I buy a long woman's shirt-blouse, which I wear after my friend's wife has taken it in at the waist and chest.

I receive a letter from the theater director Antoine Vitez asking my permission to stage *Tomb for 500,000 Soldiers* in his Théâtre National de Chaillot. I send the permission to him, in an envelope, on a card where the writing spills over onto the image.

In mid-November, the news reaches me of the murder by Louis Althusser of his wife Hélène. I meet him, after the great snow-in of late December 1970, at New Year's Eve, with two other friends, J.K. and Ph.S., at the home of a common friend, Christine, whose jewels tinkle all night.

*

Last hot day in Cap Couronne. A girl, who has a shooting gallery and sells candied apples at the fairgrounds, rests between customers on a warm rock to the left of her stall and her naked legs on the edge of the path that rises from the beach: her large, faded pink mouth, her jaws protruding into a muzzle, squeezed into a white rag filthy with frying, her breasts, large and fresh, bouncy, squeezed into a rag of the same cloth held up by tattered snippets that are knotted in the back; shorts made of the same rags squeeze, squeeze the pale scarred thighs, squeeze, unbuttoned, a fat cunt with its fat curled up, wild, labia minora.

At night, in the coming storm, I hear something like an animal dragging across my truck; at dawn, outside, I get a whiff of a mark running along the right side, on the tailgate, the left, I smell it, it is what my Algerian friends then call "cramouille," and what I taste and drink long ago from the slit of my concubine.

Marseille, Pointe Rouge, a Friday night of the following week; I want to find a young workman whom I have seen perking up, Wednesday, from his hole in the road and casting around his generous haunches, eye riveted to mine, from behind the fence.

Leaving my camping-car on the Vieux-Port, I take the bus to the construction site.

From behind the fence, from the small window in a cabin on stilts where the lights are still on, a curly face smiles at me; I am very lightly dressed in the humid cold, and very skinny; I roll myself a cigarette, take my time and do not move an inch; the guys come out, good laughs, good paunches, good pay? I shake, not from the cold but from anticipation; I light the cigarette; the door, the small staircase, squeaks, he jumps into the mud, his scarf, very long and thick, gets caught beneath his shoe and his stocky body stumbles: I see, between his two coattails, his jeaned haunches split by the light of the moon, I push the construction site door, go to help him get up; the key to the construction site is in his front pocket; his fingers bloodied from the fall, nose pitted to the ground, he can't reach; I grab the key from his pocket—his meager belongings packed against his now erect member—and lock the Algeco; inside me and on my lips: *"Before the sun goes down tonight, you and I will be together, in your bed or in mine"* (in churches, always, the beauty of the good thief, Saint Dismas).

Farther into the city, in a corridor coming back from dropping the key into a mailbox in a courtyard, I take his nostrils in my mouth and suck the blood.

Very sleepy but egged on by the member, we walk through Bonneveine toward downtown: oysters and red meat near the sea. Since he cannot, or will not, return at this hour to the house of an uncle of his father's side where he is staying, somewhat separated from the house nonetheless, he leads me, in a large warehouse area under renovation, up to a high building, gray and red, with a broken window from which tattered strips of black and khaki covers hang and flap. In a long hall with cast-iron pillars, where parts of the wood floor are rotting upon black earth, silhouettes, young, bundled up, err from one pillar to another. At the end, on raised flooring and near a hole that a plank runs through—water, underneath, toilets or the sea?—are five, seven mats where other bodies sleep under covers, except for arms, bandaged or not.

Still farther, in a high-ceilinged shanty with a jutting angle, my foot hits upon three mats; we lie on one, fully clothed, beneath a busted comforter... the blood from his nostrils is dry.

Awake before dawn, I get up and walk, very slowly, in the direction of a glow: in another shanty, symmetrical to ours, is a crouching boy with a gray fake fur hat and red cheeks warming his hash with a knife; in front, on the mat, legs spread wide, those of a girl, and, the cover pulled up, the same cunt squeezed into the same rag; the same rag on the mouth sleeping and blowing a trickle of snot; the same grimy strap squeezing the same breasts, avid for life, for giving...—"*what a bundle, brother, I see you want some, go ahead, do her, it'll wake her up for work...*"

... late 1970, I am having lunch with Michel Leiris at the Totem, the restaurant located at the Musée de l'Homme; while we are having dessert, Jean Rouch comes over to our table, accompanied by Lillian Gish, the actress, with French ancestry, who plays in *The Wind*, *Intolerance, Broken Blossoms...* Michel tells her what I am; she tells him that she finds me attractive, and, speaking about a great actor from heroic times, explains that all the women desired him, but that he had none... My cheek still warm from the kiss she gives the lost children in *The Night of the Hunter*, I am filled with such dread, later, as I walk through the Trocadéro Gardens, alone!...

In the municipal baths where we shower in two faraway stalls of the rotunda building, his wound reopens, I must, in the street, suck it again.

I buy him jewels: necklaces and earrings, silver and coral; I fasten three necklaces one to the other in the tender folds around his waist, necklaces that he wears, beneath the high-waisted jeans, when he takes me with him to his uncle's restaurant in the Panier; I propose to rewrite the menu; surrounded by children back from a party, and intent on the necessity to renew, in my notebooks, with the figures at hand, I write, under the blackening stare and the knotting brow of the young workman:

> *Noureddine chops*
> *— Noureddine heart*
> *— Noureddine thighs*

*— Noureddine shoulder*
*— N'... loin taken from the bottom of Noureddine's*
*haunches as a balls-to-ass backseat rider on a motorcycle*
*— Red mascara to paint Nour's eyelashes with.*

\*

I buy a new camping-car with the sale of the old and with my share of the sale of our house. I nurse the project of living as a true nomad from my new truck. My anxiety clings to all that affixes, to dwellings, to foundations, to furniture. I feel that even the nonviolent revolution that I still hope for at the time is incompatible with the binding of peoples and of individuals to the soil where they were born.

To nomadize is to make oneself available to all, to those who are close to us but especially to strangers.

It is also to forget the self, increasingly; the self that is the true enemy and that still remains, unfortunately— and for how long—the backing of creation.

It is thus easier to enter the economy and intimacy of human groups if one transports, in one's work vehicle, the people, and their food and goods.

As long as my communist commitment lasts, having learned to see with the first images of the death camps, I rule out the violence of revolution and yet the revolution is, for me, a new man, with new sentiments, and perhaps as well, if I carry the whole thing to its logical conclusion, a disappearance of feeling that might begin with the inversion of feelings, their subversion. The depth of that movement, even though it hurts me, is plain to see if you pause an instant on what the work I do shows and proves: a world overturned.

To do so I start sleeping in my day clothes. Added to my desire for social availability is the fear of being found dead, and being buried in my nightclothes. To be at war, ready to break camp or to affront death in full possession of one's identity and social power.

My dreams, as powerful then as sleep is short (the need to buy time against the return of illness, for work), intimate that a departure of sorts is close at hand, demand that I live all my time awake, or that an eternal dream engulf my entire being.

As long as you are thinking, you cannot die. Thus, as a child, when I do not want something to happen, I repeat to myself or murmur: "*It will happen, it will happen, it will happen...*" For it to happen: "*May it not happen.*" Even at the time, thoughts and words must accompany, cover, dominate the event to come; it is often in moments of *inattentiveness* that the worst has befallen me.

As a child, I mostly proffer this magical language about what others are about to experience. So that now, at the end of the year 1980, I long for things to accumulate in this darkening close of the year, for day to be longer than day, for night—during which I work as well—to be longer than night, time longer than time. Dread that life might escape words, that it might escape the vigil I keep and with which I accompany it.

Certain enchanting, bewitching forms of music lull me to sleep for a few seconds—sleeping during the day is one of the greatest terrors of my life.

Because each note, each chord provokes powerful images in me; thus my heart, as an organ, almost grows hallucinated. The music itself develops, during those few seconds, five, seven—I hear it, I even see it on the score—it segues in a melodic line, in chords, rhythms that are not in the real score. When I wake from that very brief slumber, the real music, for its part, has advanced only five or six notes. In the brevity of its own real time, uncontrolled by me, I can measure the brevity of my sleep. Such sucking in, of my organism almost whole, by nothing but a few sounds, albeit organized, which then ebbs toward the unknown, literally breaks my bones. This fall of sorts, within myself, as is the very beginning of sleep, wrenches my insides. Who grabs them? The housewife does not wring her kitchen towel dry with greater strength.

Night sleep, by its duration, appeases the horror of its first jolt.

There is a kind of imbalance between how small we are athletically and the enormity of the cerebral network of which we are the seat, and the enormity of the impulse toward the more that we are through the heart. The skeleton, the organs themselves are worth nothing. What is of value is the network.

Today—but is it only today?—the thing in itself, what is intrinsic no longer counts, only the consequences count: whether it is of an event, a being, a person, an idea, an object, we only see consequences. The being of a thing, its origin, the movement toward what preexists even morality, toward a before-"God"—which would explain why remorse is so terrible, and so impossible at times—are neglected because they cause fear or require thought. Ideologues themselves, those who are labeled philosophers and who probably suffer from this disappearance of being, do not deal with being but with society in which beings must cope. Action is forgotten as well. It seems that the only thing that counts are the words with which all people manifest that they wish to stay away from being or action.

14

At the end of December 1980, I meet with my brothers and sisters in the village where we were born. Despite the bitter cold, I refuse to spend the night inside the house. I want to live in my camper loaded with the presents I am going to distribute. Instead of parking the van near my father's last house, on the river, away from the village center, where his second wife still lives, and where everyone is gathered, I park in the center of the village, in front of the old building where all of us were born, and where our mother died on August 25, 1958.

The sweet, deliberate insomnia, my freedom of movement and my distance from the complexity of the family, the typewriter, the *Samora Machel* notebooks, the hand-writing in them still regular and very readable, open on the small working table, set before a large window giving onto what landscape I choose, a good engine almost beneath my feet, a loved figure in my heart and mind, master of all time—sleep, dreaming almost abolished, why be concerned about the restlessness they see in me?

I no longer see obstacles, I no longer see adversaries. What I experience as a new lightness is the loss of my weight. The beauty of winter, its light, the brilliance, the sparkle of snow and ice, the purity of the air (the theater production planned for December at Chaillot) create a kind of glorious body (cryogenization) with which I can cross that forty-first year of my life, that year, added to the one that I had, in adolescence, decided would be my last; all the while, pneumonia, mycoses take possession of my body, in that vehicle where I begin to hoard goods and cans, but where I hardly eat now.

On the road to Paris, just behind the vehicle in which my brother, his wife and their young two-year-old are riding, my happiness is so great that I must sometimes stop the van and get out to place my fingers in the tracks of animals and people, wash down my Compralgyl—an analgesic available over the counter at the time—with snow, observe a crow, a magpie, a thrush; as night falls, around La Charité, I suddenly feel like trying out the roof that opens like a tent.

In Orléans, I park my vehicle at the foot of my brother's building. I sleep there. Some of his Arab friends come visit and people see me working there; they complain to my brother, and, for other reasons as well, I have to leave, in a hurry.

\*

Driven out of Orléans, I return to Paris, which I had left at the end of July 1980. I go back to my small run-down studio and, far from the sheltering splendor of the great outdoors where I spent nearly three seasons, begin to experience the truth, then the reality of my exhaustion.

Before leaving again and renewing with that dream of writing in front of all possible landscapes, surrounded by friendly people, eyes on the animals on the other side of the glass or outside the vehicle, I need to build up my strength, at least what is necessary for that steadfast central force, but methodically.

My downstairs neighbor, a friend, deformed from the waist up, who works as a gardener, French on his mother's side and Kabyle on his father's, something of an actor or harlequin from Picasso, decides to help me get back in shape, he brings me, for lunch and dinner, to a cafeteria at the edge of the Fourteenth Arrondissement.

Lean fish, on my plate, in a light that illuminates us like Rembrandt's *Emmaus*.

During that regeneration, which I believe is short, I work with regularity. But slowly, the duplicates of my central figure, Samora Machel, who was already toiling, at work, sexually, in the writing done in Aix in January–February of the previous year, turn filthy; naked figures act in increasingly degraded places, space is further reduced.

From Algeria, Corsica, Sardinia, Marseille, the Goutte-d'Or, the stage moves up to the industrial and mining northern slope of the massif (Pilat) from whose bucolic southern slope I hail. Pigs mingle into human sex. The setting of the story shrinks to what appears to be the coal shed in the courtyard of the building in which we lived when I was born, and where, as a child, I imagine a world lies, alive under the pile of shiny nut coal.

In the end, not only do the pigs have coarse hair on their greasy skin, but the prostitutes too, and one of them is called Anthracite. Actions and words are resorbed in a sweet, generous, plaintive, repetitive chant; for which a series of a few words, interjections... suffice.

Such is the tempting sweetness of that chant that again I cannot bear to interrupt it—if I stop, I am dead and damned by Nothingness. But the anguish I feel rising again within me is such that I must leave.

\*

One last night, I go up the Goutte-d'Or, park my vehicle there. At a barbershop which opens late, and where I am supposed to pick up the documents for a new immigrant, an illegal alien, so that they can be transformed into a residence permit by a friendly cousin of mine at the office of the Prime Minister, my eyes catch those, black-red in a bluish white, of a young worker, through the spray vaporized over his head by the barber.

I squat down on the linoleum and pick up a handful of his hair:—"*For Samora*," I whisper.

Outside, we go into a couscous joint, at the foot of a ramp, to gulp down a loubia in which he dips a lot of bread.

Where does he sleep? in a hostel? in a furnished room? if, his foot on mine, he delays our departure, it is because he doesn't dare bring me where he sleeps; but I insist, I know it is one of those places where Samora is *ordered forward*, pushed, taken and *joyfilled* till dawn.

A corridor full of rough, soft men who smoke, children in pajamas or shorts, who run after each other; a wood partition along the deep, low and yellow room of a café; at the end of the corridor, the stairs; under the stairs, what used to be a coal shed: he looks for the key to the padlock which secures it; I grab him by the shoulders and the waist, make him laugh, to shake his embarrassment—perhaps his shame, and drown it in our naked embrace!

In the coal shed, a mattress and a formica chair appear in the light of a portable lamp, strung to the end of a wire which runs, beneath the door, all the way to the very smoky room where a song is slowly ascending amid the commotion.

He makes me squat and sits me on the mattress, he leaves and comes back with a hot teapot, two tinted glasses, sugar and a bunch of mint; both our necks bent against the low ceiling ..., "*for, after all, what else is there... when near a lair?*"

The next evening, here he is in my room:—"it's not much bigger than my place." Since he is struggling to sew the crotch of his jeans, torn on the building site, I do it for him; I have him read a story on the siege of Constantine, the nerve center of the region he comes from—a douar on the massif where, in the past, I carry food products from one family to another in the desert.

After the embrace at the far end of the room—*"you are so skinny, I'll get you to eat, you'll see!"*—that spills over onto the reloosed tiles, he wants to collect his dirty shoes on the other side: I squat, on all fours, bite and push them toward the mattress where he dresses slowly, yawning, scratching his beautiful scarred buttocks, marked by all those things that can hurt a child from the mountains.

Outside, in the late Saturday night, on a vacant lot off Avenue du Maine, he pulls a flute from his fake fur-lined jacket and plays:—*"The rats are too deep, in this frost, to come out and follow you."*—*"What if I find all of the wicked and lead them to the Mosque?"*

*

Restlessness returns: I must hurry toward what's killing me.

Appeasement through regularity is starting to grow on me and frightens me (only a new situation in a new place, mobile if possible, changing, can bring me peace), I travel to see an actor friend in Reims: he is playing in *Monsieur de Pourceaugnac* and recites: *"plenty of stratagems."*

In the theater restaurant, I want to try some of those pig's ears that, twelve years earlier, I play at setting behind my ear (against the petrosal bone), then masticating. I search the menu for snout as well. In the sequences I am writing at the time, bodies are reduced to a mouth, a snout, perhaps a voice and sound that come out of them.

I park my van on a curve of the small street, rue Hincmar, that is named after the bishop from Merovingian times; near the gate of the house and garden of the costume designer of the play.

It is bitter cold.

One evening, at dinner, I begin to lose consciousness. On a bench of the square in the town center, lying down, I see moving clouds.

My friend, who is staying at the hotel facing the square, takes me upstairs, where I will sleep on a bed, at the far end of the main room.

My body feverish—cockroaches in the shower—I read a book he has given me as a present: Peter Härtling's *Hölderlin*, in Philippe Jaccottet's translation. Hölderlin's figure, with some lines of the "tower poems" which I've known by heart since adolescence, substitutes itself as a ghost in my body, to which fever alone provides a contour and strength.

For the final days, I park my van in the costume designer's garden. I sleep there sheltered from the wind and in an intensified cold. The workroom where she lives is warm, colorful materials impart a light that tarries at the end of the afternoon, more belated than daylight. On a less cold morning, after a shower with the hose outside, she offers me jam. Long ago, in the glorious Tamesna—a desert plateau in North Niger—the setting of the last scene of *Eden, Eden, Eden*, the jam made from the gum sap of the acacias ...

One late morning, I take my friend to Attila's camp, first a Gallic redoubt, then Roman, and finally Hun. The vehicle gets stuck in the mud on the edge of the ellipse-shaped arena on the banks of the Noblette River: my friend's fear of being late and holding up the play— theater is also for me a ritual on which the order of the world could depend—fills me with such anguish that I am utterly annihilated.

# Plus passionnant que 20 romans d'aventure...

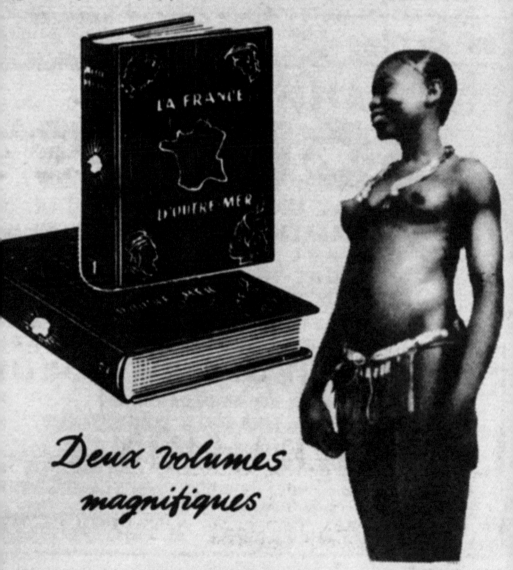

*Deux volumes magnifiques*

VOICI une chance pour vous de tenter une aventure réservée d'habitude aux millionaires : un voyage complet dans les cinq parties du Monde :

## 15

Back in Paris, in my room—by that time it has become impossible to live in a vehicle in Paris—as if fueled by the need to see, to the best of my abilities, all that can be seen awake, to see more, almost, than the time of day and night, I decide, despite the thinning, diminution and softening of the mucous membranes and membranes of my body—the eye resists—to try soft contact lenses. I shall wear them day and night without interruption.

I struggle to distinguish, from the convex, the concave side to set upon the eye. I wear the lenses overnight not knowing which side is in. The pain is very strong at dawn, I paw at the lenses and peel them off like skin. My eyes burn me like long ago, at Thebes in summer 1965, the sun burns them through the magnifying glass of my hard contact lenses.

I have to wait nearly a month to wear my hard lenses again. But till then, once the bandages around the eyes are off, I have to wear the glasses through which, as a young adolescent, the world appears reduced, drab, lackluster— but this, in order to transfigure it through writing.

Fatigue, vague vision make me walk and move slowly now, and the more the writing in the notebooks contracts—the letters grow taller and their line resembles a medical chart—drops from left to right, and finally disappears—the text continues in my head, in my organs and limbs—the more my voice grows slow, deep, and the stuttering of childhood resurges with a vengeance.

When I am in a store, at the cashier, I must prepare inside my throat the sentence of inquiry that I will make, anticipate the short commentary, and what and how to answer it, choose the words to anchor the beginning, middle and ending of my sentence, repeat those lines several times, place my hand in such a way on the counter so as to stress the issue of the sentence; place my foot on the ground so that I may exist, appear as something other than a ghost.

My feet and legs, swollen because of the heating system in the van, start to feel the way thighs feel beneath the fingers after general anesthesia: dead, rubbery, barely sustaining the half of my weight, which I have shrunken to.

My skin up to my hands grows covered in mycoses, my toenails grow and curl beneath the flesh. My hands shake, I must contain the shaking of one with the pressure of the other.

The search for Compralgyl, which I take increasingly, close to a hundred pills a day near the end of the year, is such that almost all my movements are linked to it: taking the pills, storing them even, requires that I hide from those closest to me, that I invent exceptional situations. The only way I take the pills now is dry. Searching for them is an ordeal; that ordeal keeps me upright. I garner my strength to walk, to take subways and trains toward pharmacies I have not yet visited; in those where I have already made a purchase, I conceal myself in the longest lines and order, as if covertly, with a casualness I think beguiles; in the pharmacy in the Galerie des Champs-Élysées, open twenty-four hours a day, I wait for groups of tourists to mingle in with them, and place my order in their accent. But my stutter, which is then very strong, forces me into internal and external contortions that I imagine, I tell myself for comfort, will induce in the salesclerks either mockery, indulgence or distraction; roaming the suburbs by train, on foot—I fear buses for they compel a greater intimacy—

shadows hide bodies I no longer desire; I lose myself there at times.

There, one late afternoon, I take a shortcut, the ache for Compralgyl egging me on, walking between two parallel train tracks, stepping over the hot rails—hot enough to roast a rat. A train skirts me, then another in the opposite direction.

At times, people hit me; in railway stations, where I am detained near the platform. Who hits me? And with what authority? Policemen, fathers, employees? I feel no anger whatsoever. My bones alone call for justice; because of the way I am, it is never "I" that is insulted, beaten, pushed away, but, in my self, something of the surface, a physical, interdependent reality, or an historical, even metaphysical solidarity; the only feeling, the only thought I have ever had of myself is as a medium, an intermediary, a messenger. And I have always been greatly loved as such, as the one who brings light or who restores it to the heart of another.

And yet, save for what tortures me, the artistic solution to be found, nothing wounds me more in the brief recurrences of my emotional self than the incapacity of others, sometimes those closest to me, to see, to understand the effort that I extend to live, to renew with life.

The tiny, incremental progress that has me quivering with joy, no one can discern: it is so interior, almost atomic in scale, that no one can detect it without the help of a microscope. I know only too well the secret of the internal progression of an idea, an image, a figure, to doubt the reality of these improvements; and too often, and for so long, I have seen in other people the spectacle of their interior transformation that I cannot but feel the injustice of judging them always on what is fixed.

It hurts that people closest to me look at me with the same eyes as yesterday (but no matter, we must push onward): the very idea of infinitude is affected.

For the first round of the May 1981 elections, I have to vote by proxy because I am still registered in my native village; policemen from the 14th Arrondissement come to pick me up at home, I fill in the usual paperwork in front of them at the police station: they bring me back, holding me up by the arm, and thank me for having taken the trouble to vote in my condition.

The day after the results, returning from the house of some close friends on the other side of the Seine, I am caught in a storm, under the foliage of the Jardin du Luxembourg: I feel I have climbed, through heavy and obscured valleys, past the Gare de Lyon and the boule-vard Saint-Michel, a steep incline reaching a plateau of great enchanted greenery.

The merry-go-rounds are still running, children and families under cover. I climb into one of them as it slows down, and settle into a kind of golden bowed dinghy, brimming with rainwater, I let myself sink in and doze off in the warm water.

The merry-go-round has stopped; I climb out of the water at nightfall. The gilded wooden fish on the bow looks at me—a fish, so high up?—the rain has stopped, I spread my canvas jacket on a bench; I feel the weight I've lost through the remaining clothes sticking to my skeleton.

I come and go then, without the sensation of clothes or nudity.

One May evening, I am at a rehearsal of Hölderlin's *Empedocles*, in the suburbs where *Eden, Eden, Eden* was written not long ago, I see an old friend, M., mouthing his text from the top of a cardboard mountain, and transfigure him into Job sitting on the heap of his feces. At the time, I defecate with greater difficulty than usual in the toilets on my landing, Turkish toilets with the water frozen over in winter and, in summer, the worms rising from the hole: I sometimes feel that I am defecating skins from my throat and from my tongue, and then my tongue itself.

Time grows distended: in the Boucheries Bernard where I stock up on what I will not eat, all kinds of food are on the shelf, the space resembles a gorge or an underground cave where quarters of meat rotate, suspended in the back, like bloody ex-votos in an underground basilica. So is Monte Sant'Angelo in the Gargano, spring 1980. From a fruit stall, on my right, a coconut falls onto the tiles and shatters. The sound of the fall comes to me long after the smell of milk; far away—will I have enough strength, there, to have a voice, to turn and twirl the sentence in my mouth, to order the meat?—under the neon lights, as if upon a stage, bonneted officiants, something like a buzzing of pounded mallets, the musical grinding and clinking of blades, the smacking of flesh being pounded at the blocks, am I not that Inca child, chosen along with others, whose thinking flesh is sacrificed, up there and away?

One night, before dawn, having bought large quantities of chopped meat and milk, I put them in a mesh bag along with some small saucers and small silverware, and go down to the Parvis de la Tour Maine where some drifters tend a fire under a metal scaffolding.

Afraid of falling asleep at night, and being captured by death in sleep, I stay awake, inside or out: searching for Compralgyl and slow walking keep me outside for a large portion of the night. At times, when I have gone to bed at dawn upon my return, the anxiety of day emerging from that of night, I shed my clothes, dress in that same woman's blouse I wore last summer, and sit, legs underneath me, on the mattress laying directly on the tiles at the far end of the room, drawing to myself objects of daily use as well as some small necklaces, pendants with hands of Fatima, small lighters, and other miniature objects. Around my neck I hang the little chain that we, soldiers in Algeria, all wear around our neck, with our army serial number engraved on the brass for identification in case of death in action, and add to it the little nickel silver and silver-plated necklaces that I have bought in the Goutte-d'Or some time ago, or that the little sisters of my friends have given me.

One afternoon, a friend, finding me thus and knowing nothing of my night walks, speaks of me as *bedridden* just as he had done the winter before At the time, I am writing my *Samora Machel*—ensooted and multiplying into as many doubles as my lost flesh demands protectors— attached with belts to the chair my father has given me, and that I have painted red, so that I might stay awake at my work table. The word pierces me all the more because the bed in the sequences I am writing designates the pallet on which are tested my enslaved and joyous figures.

During that spring, which is spring only for others, the word lacerates me all the more, for in this cruel season I try at times to give to my experience, if not meaning, at least, for me alone, for my own conscience, a slightly noble image, and thus I try to raise, to elevate my unrespectable distress to the pain of Job, and see myself on his dung heap rather than on the bed of the normal sick to which the adjective *bedridden* refers; just as the noun is beautiful, the adjective is ugly. Knowing the value of words, I take this adjectival transformation to be a reduction of my suffering, its regulation, its hospital normalcy.

Early July, invited for dinner, I climb with difficulty to the home of the young woman, the lady friend with whom I lived for two years, ten years before, she, then, very young and very desirable, with a good heart and very lively spirit, I, at the end of *Eden, Eden, Eden*: happy times, friends visit often, we travel, but fearing, perhaps, it's in the air, that by wrecking her, I might wreck what makes me live—create—she refuses me her main entry, which my member desires, and deviates it toward her mouth, toward her voice; I can satisfy her only with my tongue, and only with my fingers. Does she betray me when she falls into the arms and underneath the members of others, I, who refuse to force her and will suffer this lack of completion to no end?

In all my adult life, this is the only moment I experience a common regime because I am not writing.

I do not remember if I stay over, greeted with such tenderness and cheer.

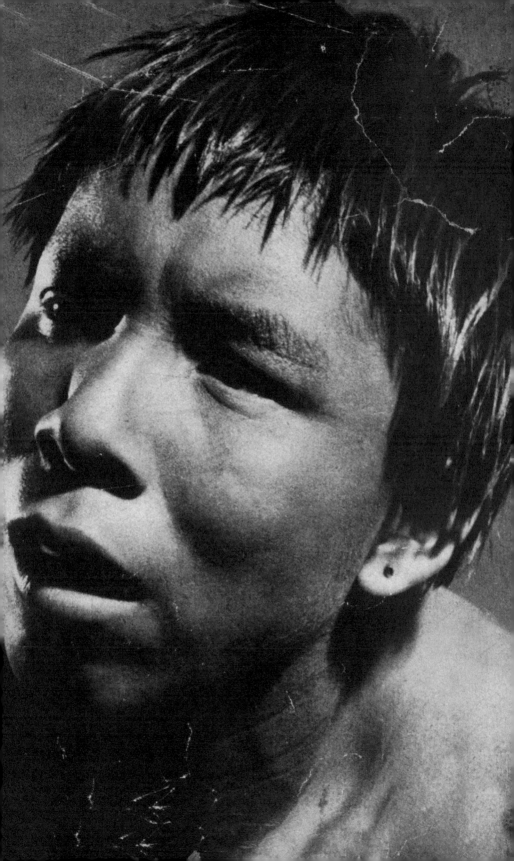

# 16

One night after falling asleep in terror, I dream that our mother, my mother, meets *me* (but *who* are *we* in dreams?) on the Parvis de la Tour Maine: destitute, wearing the rags of good prewar dress— sable—in the state of abandon that she reaches during the last weeks of summer 1958, when we carry her— who is that in her arms, our father, us, her children, a visitor? in an easy chair to the garden where, exhausted, arms upon the armrests of the chaise longue, alongside the shadow of the pines, in the flight of insects and the rumble of the torrent below, she is most beautiful, most beautiful—and has thus remained, for me. But here, at night, upright, she walks toward the low wall around the flowerbed.

As I ask her to take me back, for she would know what might make me live again where I must...— *"mother, take me back!" (to nonexistence, because, even if you were to abort me, my human soul, recreated through you, would join a new hell)—she tells me, "ask your father, my sweetheart."—"he too is dead..."—"go find him, my sweetheart."* Dream again to look for my beloved father—and to find him, but in what condition... but she disappears.

I wake from the dream with a cry, return to the Parvis de la Tour Maine, inquire if the drifters have not seen her. I wait for the dawn, quick to come in that season, on the low wall, walking around the flower bed where birds pick up their song in the growing noise of cars, then trains, tremor of the ground, then, en route to Compralgyl!

*

The next day, a late July afternoon—during that month I have received a personal letter from the new President inviting me to his garden party at the Elysée, although a phantom, I do not go but still attend—I walk to the home of my friends B. and Z. at the top of the 11th Arrondissement, under the

Couronnes subway station. It is a very long space in a high industrial building.

He is a painter, who makes a living on construction sites, and Z. works in an administration and writes.

They often invite me, I feel at home with them—they often come to my place. During the summer, large windows open onto the crowded street, which could easily rise from the Bosphorus, with shopkeepers, artisans, working as much outside as in, oriental neon signs, pastry display cases laden with everyday objects, automobiles, bicycles, made of sugar…

Two thirds of the place are in the dark, spots of colors, forms emerge from my friend's canvases swept by the lights and glow of the street.

The rest, two large glassed-in alcoves, the kitchen, and across from it, the bedroom, in which their child T. has been sleeping since early spring.

I have almost lost weight because of the dream about my mother and what it has provoked. That evening, out of revolt against all that is forsaking me (my mother's God, my mother herself—God's will for me and grace: must I withstand the test of all true artists, of the gesture of their spirit, which designates their exception, that cruel passage without the assistance of He who wanted what I am, and of she who carried me to become it), I feel as if I were ejecting, vomiting through my mute mouth the inverted remains of my body, with its memory, its ancient and future actions, its disappearance.

I latch onto the newborn asleep in the gleam of the night-light, I grasp onto its faraway odor, and its mewling, onto the faraway, changing odors of its tossing in the crib.

Dinner over, after having read a dazzling text of hers, afraid of renewing, in a dream, with my even more destitute mother, Z. leans over me on the couch where I sleep: it is as if Algeria, its war having made me anew long ago, were leaning over me again, now undone, and trying, at least, to have me sleep dreamless.

It is Z., it is, at a further remove, Egypt, Zuleika, the wife of the eunuch Potiphar, seductress, temptress of Joseph, temptress of the Joseph who is sold by his brothers and in whom, as a child, I have always recognized myself since the time accompanying my father on his medical rounds, when he had asked me to interpret his dreams, and thus, despite himself, had ushered me into poetry and away from himself—from his dislocated body he asks me again, in a slight delirium, before dying in late 1971; I dream of myself then, on the edge of a well, a spring-cistern in a small valley in our native mountain, and with what little knowledge I possess of numbers, I calculate the price of my sale. Then, somewhere else, a tribunal of sorts demands it of me again, and I no longer remember my price.

Stretched out—all beds have now become like racks on which the torture victim is placed for renewed torture, only the upright and walking positions can liberate me slightly from my fear—I try to soothe myself, inducing the image of Samora, the first, original Samora, before the doubles, the triples that are born of him as if sprung from his thigh, like Eve from Adam's rib: although he goes naked, I try to cover him an instant in disguises, or brand him with a mark, or decorate his waist with string, in reference to the Biblical image, and Koranic image, of Joseph's shirt during his flight, a shred of which remains (is it the back or front?) in Zuleika's fist: in *Samora Machel*, what am I to do, also, with this Mark who, having come to Gethsemane for news, and following a captured Christ, escapes the soldiers, leaving the thin fabric that sheaths him in their hands? From what soldiers shall he run, the child who sleeps nearby, grown into adolescence and following what Messiah? And later, from what brothel, oh gods—for that is my duty!—shall I have him removed by the string that girds his waist and parts his ass, and lead him toward what workers?…

Later, as I tell Z. the dream I had of my mother, she worries, and, her baby in one arm, takes my hand with the other; but everything excludes me from life: life, even.

17

In July, I decide to return south to Martigues and to settle near my friends. A friend who has just learned to drive leads the way in his car. I drive fast and loose, yet flashes of brief sleep force me to pull myself together. My friend worries as he sees my head drop in his rearview mirror.

In a large rest stop north or south of Mâcon, at night—it enrages me that I cannot enjoy these places that I love—the movement of cars at arrival and departure, the voices of those who leave them and who enter them, the young sleepy children on their mothers' shoulders, the lights, large, small, steady, blinking, dazzling, veiled, the smells of gas, of hot tires, of steel, of drinks, of hotdogs. Highway signs, slogans, and ads flutter about (the powder falling from the wings of butterflies veils the whole). With the speed, within myself, of surges of hope and crashes of despair. My friend calls my younger brother H., who lives and works in the area. Here he comes. My friend cuts toward Grenoble, my brother and I drive down to Avignon. The heat grows more intense, my brother has promised to bring me to Martigues, but in Avignon I drive him to the train station where he takes a train for Paris.

Once past the feeling of my return to the world— standing among young soldiers on that station platform with its pillars still hot, with my travel and live-in vehicle outside on the parking lot and a free trip to take between midnight and dawn—as the train carries my brother, my blood, toward the north, a feeling of terror grips me that shall not loosen its hold for most of the summer.

I take the wheel and enter into a space of hostile dreams (black circuits, slides that seem like ramps, entrails where I must align myself with the extreme, aerial speed of vehicles of unrecognizable form) with levels superimposed, great roads, plains, arid hillocks and woods, black or white, compact and aligned; in the canals and rivers, hot and heavy water runs in both directions, the *entirely* starry sky is but another level, threatening to crack, of that zone through which I maneuver my yet-to-be-created home.

Through villages and suburbs arrested in the night, to flee the great roads, I lead my vehicle onto steep lanes, between houses where the lights of life have been extinguished, but where dogs keep vigil, in chains.

In Les Baux, or is it in Arles?, I turn onto a deep-set alley that ends in a precipitous fall. As I back up, my wheels skid on a sand bank, I get out, all of my bones shaking, almost raw now beneath a thin coat of flesh, and skirt to the back to get the winch used long ago in the desert to recover my other vehicle from the sand.

The coat of sand is thin, a new worksite probably. I uncover the hard bed with a small military shovel, but, as I imagine that it shall crumble at the *lifting* of the wheels, I start to dig deeper, thinking I will reach absolute firmness, this zone's original shell.

The noise completely wakes the dogs who pull on their chains. I must end it, I no longer have the build, or bone, to withstand human blows without dying. Back in the cab, I throw the motor into reverse, the vehicle flies, almost bursting, out of the dead end that opens onto the void.

Back on the road, I make several stops to assure myself that no dogs have climbed into the back of the vehicle. I double-check, going through the inside of the van, curtains drawn, from the cab to the living compartment and the work area, I lift the blankets, the sleeping bag, the books, the notebooks, fling open the cabinets whose collection of cans has grown since my last purchase at the rest area, purchases I will continue to make during the remaining half of the summer. No dogs.

But in a village, where a spike of terror has made me stop and step out of the van, settle on a bench in the middle of the central square with its circle of insect-veiled street lamps, here they come lunging from all convergent avenues. As they pause, suddenly, in their charge, a cry rips out that I think might free me, but terrorizes my own limbs instead. The dogs bolt in the opposite direction.

At dawn, disengaging my vehicle from the sand once more, on the banks of the Étang de l'Estomac, I emerge from between the high facades of the refineries and cement factories of Fos and follow the gulf, thinking I am on the other side, on the Berre side, on the northeast border of the water (Marignane). The sea is that same blue in which, as a child, I imagine the Greek underworld lies, with its judgments, its submarine scales, its dog Cerberus. Am I not one of those heroes, semi-gods, future celestial bodies, children borne of goddesses and men, of gods and women, or of women and beasts, momentarily led back to the surface and to life by its judgment?

I no longer know what I am driving, a van or an ancient chariot.

I arrive at the home of my friends very early, and cannot hide the terror which I inhabit.

Outside, living on the same spot as the year before, on the southern side of the Étang de Berre, I shall experience several days of black light, the lines of the landscape, of the buildings, of the vehicles and objects lined with red.

One evening, one night, we eat in a gas station diner after seeing the show *Le Bal*, in which, as I transform myself into each of the numerous dancing figures, I hope to explode in them that "I" which tortures me—grown more ferocious as it has shrunk. The very black tar beneath our feet, mine swollen in rat-skin moccasins— long ago, in my native village, Nanet the "drunk," leaving his cabin in the spring and coming to the village center to sing love poems beneath the windows of his beloveds (many among the village women desire him in secret), come summer, lies on his back, on the edge and also in the almost convex middle of the overheated road that crosses the village, singing more rugged songs, finally uprooting his back and ass from the heat-softened tar...

... later, some weeks before my enlistment in Algeria, during a long summer night, as I have no money, I walk, from our father's house, over the twenty-five kilometers of mountains and valleys between Déôme and the gorges of the Loire, to meet, unannounced, the girl, S., whom I very strongly desire; the following night, somewhat drowsy myself—but I must *have* her that night!—she, fresh and just out of the flock of brothers and sisters, each as tender of flesh and red in the cheek, we are on the top of a large hill, on a small, freshly tarred road, surrounded by stars; she sits in the middle, I am cross-legged across from her on the embankment, she lifts her skirt, listens to me, plump hand on her inclined cheek, her curls open raw on the softened tar and catch there, my heart skips all over…

… lizards on the rocks, long ago on the coast of Brittany, escaping from the caulking pitch where they have left their tail (there is such suffering for me, just as mysterious as scandal, in that moving image of the cruelty of the world—both so perfect and so unjust), running on the rocks, body severed and oozing a dreadful substance. And how to reconnect the whole, faster—the child is so rushed—than nature can grow a tail… but vacation will be over then, and we will have returned to boarding school…

At the pumps, guys' hands on girls' asses stuffed back into cars, brawls: they at least have a heart—for fighting, or even for killing.

Across from me, my friends, their friends, they are of another species, or rather, they belong to a species: I, myself, belong to none.

One late morning, my friends are probably having lunch with others in their house, I drive my vehicle to a supermarket to buy more cans of food. As I back up to leave the parking lot, I knock against the bumper of a fairground truck, the owners immediately rush out, insult me, hit me, throw me down, trample my head on the ground. Some policemen, who have seen the small collision and my great weakness, push them back and stop them. One of them gets behind the wheel of my van; others follow in their squad car. They drive me back to where I live, and make me drink some coffee from their thermos. For an instant, I return to social existence. They offer me their support, a number where I can call them if I am attacked or have a medical emergency.

They leave; I advance toward the edge of the water to take a piss, out of contentment but with great difficulty (my kidneys are racked by the phenacetin of the Compralgyl).

A rock is loosened beneath my swollen foot. I tumble down ten meters through the bushes. I protect my skull with my hands as I reach the first rocks that strike against my back. It takes me more than two hours to climb back up the slope.

When my friend comes out of the house to see me, I am breathless on the running board of the van, shredded T-shirt, brambles on my skull and in my ears and mangled back.

Later during the week, when the family has gone for lunch somewhere outside the city, my friend returns early to find me on all fours, in the bathroom, a branch sticking out from my ass, diddling inside my anus and trying in that way to extricate the feces that have grown more and more compact. I am not surprised by his shock, nor does it hurt me. Through the open window, I see the mulberry tree I gave them last year as a present, growing in the small garden near the water, I see, almost on the level of my crouching body, the powdery trail leading long ago to Dauphiné, to our farm called The Plan—where, as a child, I see old Tobie under the guise of a farmer sleeping, mouth ajar beneath the flight of swallows, lying under the awning of the barn—flanked by mulberry trees heavy with fruit and strewn with goat droppings; I hear the sloshing of the udders between the legs of the goats and smell the milk, which, along with the blood rising to my mouth and in my nostrils, dissolves the smells of the bathroom.

*

Where to go? I follow the route toward Aix, and climb toward my friend's place. Near it, outside, during these last few years, I write a large part of *The Book* and *Tales of Samora Machel.* I go no farther than the courtyard adjacent to his studio: beyond it lies the low altitude meadow where, at the time, I labor with my figures. He sees the degradation of my body, of my movements and of my voice. I decide not to stay, and take the direction of my native village.

How was I able to drive that summer without harming myself? After leaving the highway at Andance, as I am crossing the piedmont of the Rhône, I doze off in a curve of the road, and the vehicle crashes, rock side, into a laurel, a flowered branch of which I keep in my bumper for the rest of the summer.

## 18

In the village, to which I rarely return since our father's death, I drive up to the gate outside his second wife's house; I back the van into the bottom of the garden adjoining the *far end* of our childhood garden, abandoned now: both run alongside the same torrent. Higher up on the hill named Cotaviol, partly built into the rock face, the spacious house of a friend, an Angevine widow, the sister of our mother's sister-in-law, a profound figure of that time. I do not dare show myself to her in my condition.

One of her two adopted sons, G., who trails a difficult life, comes down to see me; I walk up with him beneath the pines and cedars toward that long house, red shutters and a vast playroom on the ground floor;

inside, large rooms, with wide windows, glassed-in porches, a central stairwell made of solid wood, light and polished, behind the house, the steep path, climbing to the level of the roof.

In the final weeks of the Occupation, as German troops pull back from Italy and Provence, retreating north, east and to the center of France with infamous bitterness and ferocity—several army units leaving the Rhône Valley take a shortcut along route 82, where recent Maquis combat their retreat; it is said that there are Mongols in those exasperated regimens (the medieval fear of Mongols persists, and transforms some tired, exhausted and dirty Caucasian conscripts into stragglers from the army of Genghis Khan)—we often take refuge there—to hide, as well, from the suspicion the resistance activities and the deportation of many of our own might warrant. After the Liberation, on Thursdays, our paternal Grand-mother will have us kneel, in her garden, before an enniched Virgin Mary set against a wall beyond the narrowing of the path between the magnolia and the pine grove (two years later, after a history lesson, I will imagine the assassins sent by Marc Antony besetting Cicero's litter there, to kill him and cut his hands for the Rostra of the Roman Forum) and ask Her to return them safely to us.

At the time, we also take refuge in the Châtaigneraie, a high mountain to the west of the small town, with what we have left of sugar, scarce then.

One late morning, the Germans overrun the village, we cross the central square with our mother; our father is behind us, with the other village men, hands against the wall, militiamen, their Peugeot 402 parked along the sidewalk of the square, search them. In our haste, one of my sisters has dropped her doll at the door of the building, and wants to go back to fetch it, with screams and tears.

Why take refuge in that house, the bottom of whose garden adjoins the top of ours? It is because, contrary to the narrow fourth-floor apartment that we rent above our father's office, and the village post office—a decisive spot in times of war—that large villa set among large trees, with comfortable depths, natural escape routes, ground floor and underground, and a solid build, seems more secure to our mother. One morning, the Germans on our doorstep and all of us, upon hearing their boots knocking at our door, lying on our stomachs under the beds in the "girls' room" at the far end of the apartment, she is able to keep them away by speaking to one of them in Polish, her native tongue.

I can now rest there, and listening to what G. tells me of his life, failed in his opinion, I can finally encourage him to live. I remember seeing him at the end of the war, with his brother, young children taken from an orphanage in Saint-Etienne, crouching and clasping one another in a large corner of the upstairs living room, and violently contracting at the slightest caress. Forced into that corner by adult contact, those two children teem with tension, emit a kind of energy that is as strong as all the war from which we are just emerging.

\*

During the night, since my insomnia continues, I leave the van, walk toward the village along the torrent whose banks are named after our father, and whose noise on the rocks, during my childhood, rises up to my bedroom above like the murmur of God preparing His Creation in jaws and saliva. I cut across the area, the cobbled section of highway—named after our grandfather, a doctor like his son—that narrows as it runs through the town center. I pass before my grandfather's memorial and climb up to the cemetery. In the moonlight, I search for an entrance toward the top of the hill, toward the forest, insects are singing. How can I cross the wall between the cemetery and the forest where animals jump? A small tree takes root at the foot of the wall, I grab it, I climb, I fall, I climb again, I fall again, I remain seated in the moonlight, before that young tree, one branch running through the wall to the other side, toward the cemetery. Dew, on my face?, the sweat of anxiety?

Once more, against the tree: dew, on the trunk—sap? jam? my own blood? Here it is, that *horrible bush*, for real this time. I am here. I am experiencing what *they* did: but with the means at hand, my own, live, with no other model than myself, and no angels in the sky. Tortured by true doubt, without the commentary of posterity.

No one before me, and in this language, has written as I write, as I dare to write, and as it is my pleasure and my plenitude. I know that with the last pages of *Samora Machel* written in May, I can, reading them here, wake the dead that lie in this enclosure, the noteworthy and obscure, the honored and forgotten, the peasants, the workers, the children, the women. How can I grow seasoned to the reality of my language, to the language of my being before I am myself? How can I appease the fear it causes me, the fear of the Unknown? How can I accept that transitory voice whose accomplishment I hear already?

On the other side of the wall—because of my weight loss and the pills, I do not feel the sprain that shall take hold of my foot that afternoon, I suffer but one pain, this language, I know its beauty is too hard for me already, too strong, and yet it moves me within with science and pleasure, but how I would prefer to use a language directly readable by all (and yet... ).

This language exceeds my strength, it moves faster than my willpower. It shocks me, makes me blush, at other times laugh, not because it is a crazy language, but because it is the language of an artist too strong for the human being that I still am: of a prophet of myself then.

I push on to my mother and father's grave. I sit alongside the gravel of the mound. My anxiety is such that it compresses the bones of my skull in such a way that I cannot feel those, at the base of my trunk, that rest upon the rock along the grave.

Letting my body go, letting my life cross what we call death, that I no longer *see*: the solution lies beyond that crossing salvation—if it is nothing but a soul raw against society, how can a body die that loses its existence with its weight? Beyond, on the other side, the ideal Grammarian, the Decipherer and the Pronouncer, for all.

It is already hard enough that this world, my world, cannot be reproduced, because of its sexual power, even in future anthologies! but that its language, at least for a time, must also be pronounced while it is read, that is unbearable: it is unbearable as well that the simple inscription on the page, the simple reading of printed lines do not allow for understanding, for beauty! I am here, on this field of the dead, crushed by the ordinary reader I have become.

To be able to serve, to serve another, others, to be able to emerge from that torment of art (fixed) to serve again as I should, I implore it of she by whom that torment was imparted—from "God"? To serve, not in order to save oneself, but to save others. Serving (using) beauty has only ever come to me to compensate for serving others.

I write on the page of a notebook—is it writing, or is it instead a drawing, a sign, a formula? lines overlap, grow blurred like the simultaneities of a moment of thought, at the time I feel my writing is ash and that if I tip the page the ash will slide along with its meaning— the plea I bury under the gravel.

\*

At dawn, afraid of crossing the wakened town, its now populated streets, I leave through the top of the cemetery; I attempt a mental chart of the topography of the lower mountain through which I might connect to the outskirts of the town and find the house. Through paths, shortcuts, stairs on which I know I shall make no encounters. In my haste, I climb too high into the mountain, from there I see the waking village. Dogs circle around the remains of carrion they have pulled from under the bed of pine needles: I can still see the pink of their pupils in what remains of the night. I want to sit on a rock, but the stone is too hard for what remains of my behind. I tear up some moss from around a tree, and place it on the rock, and sit. The dogs have dragged the carrion, down below, near the first houses, but the fetor remains very strong. I search for the roof of Jean's house, my friend from grade school, the house of vice as it is called. I hatch the project that from him shall issue my salvation, from his vitality and kindness. I wait for smoke to rise from the chimney of that roof, and hiding at every corner, I make my way down to the now abandoned garden where, long ago, a watering can in his hand, he tramples the earth of the vegetable plot, with his clubfoot, around the vegetable plants and berry shrubs.

A gray-haired woman rests her corseted breasts upon the ramp of the second-floor window. I rehearse, inside my mouth and several times, the question that I ask, that I am able to pronounce through and through: the woman, comb in hand, cries out with a deep and phlegmy voice that Jean is dead these last ten years. I climb back to the rock, continue along the mountain flank, along the path we call the Praying Mantis, that we as children take at August's end, and where, in the growing heat—which I see but can no longer feel—I start to hope that I shall be delivered, by a few people, among them Jean; the answer his wife has just given comes back to me like a sentence pronounced by a fool, not to be believed; I am now above the factory, an ancient textile mill which now processes wood, between this factory and the torrent lies the mill, which our father bought and restored just before his death, the only property he ever acquired.

I wait for the moment when everyone will be at work, in factories, workshops, shops, offices, households, to go down to the torrent and the outskirts of the town. I don't remember how to bypass the factory buildings, and head down a kind of underground passage, a covered shaft, following a canal with falls.

Farther down, this waterway angles toward the center of the factory. If I follow the canal, I get closer to the work area, where, if I am recognized, I will be forced to speak to the workers, and the sight of my degraded body might cause injury to our dead father and mother. Should I climb back up the sloping canal: the ten meters of the covered shaft seem ten times longer and I don't remember where it ends, on which bright public square, overrun with those humans I can no longer speak to as a human.

I have to fork the bend in the canal and go straight down through the undergrowth, birds fight over a small carcass there. I take off my shoes, sit on the edge of the canal, on my bones, the bottom of my swollen legs in the current. From the jagged edge of rusted metal jutting out from amongst the moving green algae, I make a thousand knives. On the other side, birds wait.

I see their ears...

*

Back in the van, its lateral door facing the yews that line the torrent, I want to eat: I remember having opened a can of peas that night, and having swallowed two-thirds of it cold. I even have a cut from the sharp edge, still bleeding, on my lip; I search for that open can, and only find closed ones; because I remember having eaten that amount, and because only ten hours have passed since then, I think I have eaten enough and do not open any cans. One of our father's sisters, evacuated from Ravensbrück by the SS, owes part of her survival to a third of a can of peas found in the latrines of the Königsberg death camp, before her liberation by the Soviets.

As I move to the other side of the vehicle, I see the alley running in a sharp incline to the bottom of the garden where I stand: here I am again in a ravine, with a vehicle, my house, to be extracted. I want to verify the accuracy of my feeling right away, and quick, as if to forestall the hallucination, I start the vehicle against the slope. Is my foot pressing on the gas, or something else? The vehicle does not budge. The ravine is deep, and detains the vehicle, to swallow it.

I climb toward the gate, up the stairs that flank the slope, and rush down as fast as possible toward the Post Office building and its telephone booths. I follow the torrent as far as possible from the parapet. Anxiety presses down on me and I fall into a large bunch of grass growing at the foot of the wall. I continue on all fours along part of the embankment, and rise only as I reach the crossing, in the growing shadow of the cruci-fix, seven meters tall, rock and cast iron, built where the torrent plunges beneath the village into an under-ground current.

At the Post Office, I move up to the counter, confi-dent: I am certain I shall encounter at least one of the "ladies of the Post Office" from the old days, whose name, Fanget, frequent in these parts, I have given to one of Samora's masters. I lean my chest against the counter that used to tower above my head—some of the

Post Office ladies used to open the trapdoor for me and lead me to the depths of those offices where I imagine the geographic, historical world begins, here, on the wall maps, in the telephone switchboard, in the parcel, letter, telegram bins (I see those offices as a palpable shortcut of space and time; of all that I shall *one day* cover with my larger step).

Today, she exits through the same trapdoor in the counter, and, her height reduced by age, kisses me and speaks to me of my mother. I call my brother R. from one of the three telephone booths. From Orléans, he calms me down, then calls our youngest brother in the Beaujolais to have him come and fetch me here and bring me to Antibes where my oldest friend, from middle school, lives with his family. By early afternoon, my brother is here; he extricates the van from the ravine, and here we are near the Rhône: hope rushes back to me with the purring of the engine, the air, and laughter.

# 19

I do not know my friend's new house: in a room downstairs, after nightfall, pillows, books, objects appear to me in the low red light of the setting sun, as if overlaid by a chunk of obscurity, and I hear my brother explain my last few days to my friend and his wife, both doctors.

Since I left Saint-Antoine the year before and despite the degradation of my body, I have not seen a doctor. Compralgyl stands in lieu of that.

How could a doctor, even very learned, understand that my exhaustion proceeds from torture that is purely of an artistic nature? My friend, whom I meet two years into my poetic training as I begin to imagine a new language, will understand, act knowingly as a doctor, and I know his trust in other forms of medicine than ours.

On the phone with my youngest brother H., who is in D., I speak as if I were calling him from D., and he were in Antibes, then I answer him as if I were, myself, my friend from Antibes, passing through D., and speaking to myself then in O., then as him, here, speaking to my friend in O. Then I speak to my brother R. standing before me as if I were on the phone with his wife in O.

The empathy that rules me, and against which I have since childhood attempted to oppose my reason, mocks me, nudges me from one identity to another, superimposes them and places as well.

I want to spend the night in my van, parked along the hedge that borders the house along the dead end, I remove the cans to take stock of them since I have bought more at a gas station on the highway; I lay them at the bottom of the wall. My friends convince me to sleep inside the house, in a high, ochre room.

The next day, having slept only a little at dawn, I go walking in the dead end and its surroundings. The sunrise transfigures these ordinary Mediterranean landscapes, pines, flowering shrubs, cactuses, into a superior California where only superior beings dwell, their brains full of inventions, having left behind the archaic age which I inhabit: their gestures are as light as their feelings. Everything is high-level work and pleasure.

I walk toward a less inhabited place, toward a plateau of very high pines with undergrowth filled with the cries of birds back from the sea. In the back, a big iron, wood, glass building, where colonies of children still sleep perhaps, and where their hanging drawings, poems, cut-outs, constructions, are pierced by the rays of that sun in whose pink I bathe my face, through the ground-floor windows. On top of the building, inside a large square, also enclosed in windows, the same work is carried on as the production of adult masterpieces, in conducive obscurity.

One summer night in 1969, during a reprieve between my father and I, the day after a confrontation—our eyes are still red from it—my father shows me a small photo from 1939 in one of our family albums. A waterfront, with pines in the top left of the picture and a light-filled building—their hotel?—my mother dreams awake, on a pier: "*we conceived you there, the following night, your mother and I,*" my heart instantly starts racing and palpitates as if bound to another: I was, I am, in that thinking womb, before being there; *before* that human "conception," I am.

My friend wants to have me hospitalized during the day at least, in a small clinic, several hundred meters from the house, to heal at least the conspicuous lesions and have me eat again. We go up to the door of the institution. In vain.

But both of them taking turns to wrench me from anxiety, I follow him to his office downtown, and wait for him in the luxuriant gardens, she feeds me; and the oldest of their three children, my godchild, thirteen years of age, and the gentleness of children with those who suffer, I quiver with the pleasure of offering him the superfluous objects he covets. The closer I get to the end, the more I give to all, as if to lessen, reduce the distance between everybody who will live, and me who will disappear. I give as an inverse movement, contrary to what the living do as they heap the dead with bare necessities.

*

Despite some improvement, I decide to leave. G., a friend, comes to pick me up me in Marseille, where I have managed to drive my vehicle. He takes the wheel, surprised and slightly frightened by my new appearance.

The more my hopes for recovery increase—first the hope of renewing my bodily, organic strength: once that is reestablished, how can I reestablish the order of creation: it is through the artistic headway of *The Book* and *Tales of Samora Machel* that I must do so, set up my future, and not go back on the traces of my evolution to negate and eliminate it—and the more, for me, the road climbs and the landscape rises in altitude, even though after Castres we descend toward Montauban.

At my friends' home, faced with their youth—they have just married—my strength diminishes again and I am soon moving among vague forms, often white, airy, as of wedlock; my thinking as well, their laughter reaches me as if through gauze.

Outside, when driving, I expect the renewal of my brain from the clear forms of nature and of monuments; I expect salvation from the smallest unveiling of landscape, the slightest geological rift.

At the Bruniquel precipice, I feel its height to be an acceptable fall, a painless drop of my body, the very little that it is, and I imagine that I shall not feel a thing as I barely have any body left—indeed, during this whole year I have lived in it as a soul, neither body nor spirit, but soul, and to live according to the soul alone creates a separation from humanity. You can only be a soul in the beyond.

The painful coincidence, in what remains of my mind, of the two figures Brunhild and Brunehaut, the fire of the first devouring the quartered limbs of the second, suffuses the moment in which my friends enjoin me to come back to the interior.

In Rabastens on the Tarn River, nothing I see contradicts the setting of the tale that has filled my imagination for thirty years, that of two adolescents walled up alive one late summer afternoon in the eighteenth century. The two mummies of this young couple, she and he, cousins, pursuing one another in the abandoned wings of either her or his dwelling, and then slipping into an overgrown excavation, are discovered in the twentieth century, in a fairly large Renaissance room buried almost intact beneath the ruins; one sitting in an armchair, the other on the floor. The smell of that mortal chamber—where the past shuts in the present, where what precedes shuts in what follows—stays with me like the perfume of indestructible love.

*

During an outing one Sunday evening before nightfall we see *The Clash of the Titans*, which is dominated by the figure of Perseus with winged sandals. Although the audience smiles, I, on the other hand, enter this film as I will my future coma: a scene where some half-goddess, princess or human emerges from her prone body as a ghost, a transparent double erect and floating above her previous envelope...

A kind of glue, a demonic viscosity holds back the limbs and movements of humans, heroes and monsters, weighs them down, save for Perseus on Pegasus, horse, the impulse of poetry, his loins, his muscles that I now lack.

Those aerial lurches that are mine when I dream, delivered of depression and engrossed in the great work, here sweep the screen, toward Mauritania, toward Ethiopia, where some justified legend locates the birth of an ancestor on my mother's side. Blessed period when the monstrosity of Medusa's head was enough to petrify adversaries, enemies, evil itself... if only I had one under my arm, to materialize my illness and thus destroy it! And that horse of poetry rushing out of the body of an ancient beauty turned monster, decapitated by Perseus, serpent-haired Medusa of my beloved Samora who disappeared into his doubles who disappeared in May...

While monsters grow restless on the Stymphalian lake, in the toilets of the cinema where I am throwing up an overdose of Compralgyl, my interior phrase, the dialogue with my mother that comes to me when I grow too weak to speak to God, which has been my habit since childhood whenever I must act, overcome the present, that dialogue resumes, and settles over what I remember of the Greek lines, Danae's lament, shut into a floating chest on the Aegean sea with her newborn Perseus, begot from Zeus under the guise of a golden shower: *"Sleep, my baby, and let the sea sleep, let our infinite troubles sleep! O Zeus, his father, may you change our destiny! And if I have let slip a word too bold, for the love of him your child, please forgive me..."*

Figeac, anxiety at its peak: I call my brother R. from a phone booth, he is at G.'s the following noon, and, at night, brings me back toward Paris.

## 20

As a child, I stare at a speck of dust, a crumb, a pebble, a rock, till it grows animated. Since I cannot stand the apparent inertia of matter, and the very isolation of objects revolts me and makes me suffer, I want to move isolated objects by staring at them fixedly: an empty flower pot, a pitcher, an old pen.

This isolation, the contempt in which we hold those empty, useless objects fills me with a compassion of reason and sentiment that is equal, and at times superior, to the one I feel for humans and for those we call animals. The exclusion from life is unbearable; the exclusion of criminals is unbearable as well.

I take some of those disdained objects, devoid of their activity, between my hands and warm them in my fist, perhaps reanimate then, I place some in my bed at night so that they might feel loved and tied to life's most intimate current: is there anything warmer, more secret, more fragile than the inside of a child's bed? That is one of the places where the world is endlessly reborn. It is one of the hearts of the world. I have no consciousness of what an object is composed of, the world at the time is full and that plenitude is filled with its plenitude alone: flesh is nothing but flesh... It is that fear, that an object might find itself alone and bereft of purpose, come the first scientific revelations (during preadolescence: universal gravitation, the body composed of water, the "immateriality" of clouds—blue sky and History within, rock clouds, villages, settings for History, for inventions, for art, for thought, Gothic forms and Faust within) that turns into the obsession of materiality: for the luster of rocks or for the dried-out insect or for the pen cap—at first, at a remove from my hiking friends, playmates or ski companions, *in situ*, I engage in a kind of interior dialogue with objects as if to reassure them, as if pledging to ease them from their solitude and place them under my protection—for those objects that I find during the long walks we take, alongside rivers and forests, that I take back with me to slip into my cold bed in the small boardinghouse, they bring the revelations of History as well, I start to chart the history of those objects, and in the surge of my mind and heart, I pounce upon what I might learn of their origin: plastic in France between 1949 and 1952, what can a child know of it? For me then, the movement back through the study of History toward the highest Antiquity accompanies my movement through the history of the object. Later, the system of Evolution, its revelation to me, will increase and extend this sensibility to something like the non-existence of things. They are preceded with such large quantities of transformations in time, each thing an instant of time, that they barely still exist. How can we live, seeing things that do not exist, hearing sounds that do not exist, touching objects that do not exist?

Every time a kind of furious movement, the roll of origins that must be suppressed in order to let us live. Those climaxes of hypermateriality, regular, buried, during which time kills space...

All is reducible then, and to nothing, to "nothing-ness": passing through my consciousness, the infinitely small crushes the infinitely vast and vice versa: those two *movements* cancel each other in their mutual crash.

Words themselves, that bind everything, are caught, explode in that refusal, that disgust of the present-bound—so they must be transformed, saved from their fixity, from their un-depth: facing the real—itself not so—they are all liars: they must be shaken down, made to cry, since they are made for crying, singing; as for the "rest," they do not express the slightest truth: only their assemblage allows them to get closer to the "real" (emptiness?)—and the true that touches us; so, perhaps numbers alone...?

There are no such climaxes in times of deep depression, and if their memory returns to our wasted body and what remains of our mind, they seem like moments of inaccessible joy.

# 21

Back in Paris, my acute anxiety past, I inhabit my room as if it were a premortuary cave, with a spring in back, the kitchen sink which I sometimes leave on to hear the sound of water.

I enter the cold autumn and winter in this way, I still go out, streets, subways, parks, churches... I no longer feel the cold nor do I hear myself cough, the streets are deep valleys; with its balconies and terraces, the Wild building of rue Vavin rises, lit up and filled with domestic figures, like an ideal, happy vertical city; the food on the plates, the wine in the glasses, grapes, hillside plots, vineyards revert back to their original shape, animals, plants, then cows and goats.

The door stays ajar during the day, as it used to, yet

no words indicate that I am working: because of the rehearsals, and as the date of Antoine Vitez' show is approaching, many visitors congregate in the small space which I have a difficult time keeping clean; journalists who interview me there describe my condition as normal. My sisters and brothers, near and far, support me in this crossing, which is theirs as well, the crossing of our double blood that I am undertaking. My sister M. ushers out the acquaintances who crush my weakness under their strong health, and under the weight of their stone-brain.

But when I find myself alone, at night, terror surfaces again, as does revolt, I am so afraid of sleep that the fear wakes me every time, and keeps me up.

What and who to fear? Is it that I will not survive my death, and that I will no longer be able to create? Transformed by death into an animal, domestic or wild, am I afraid that what I create in my new language will be interrupted and that I will have to bark it in a doghouse, whistle it in a cage, that I will be forced to howl it in vain in the forest, or mumble it in a burrow? Is it simply that once I have passed into the beyond, onto the other side, I will lose the strength to live again elsewhere?

The following day, does anyone notice that I have cried, dry-eyed, softly and in silence, till dawn?

The feelings of spring and summer have ended: compression, crushing, objects burnt to a crisp, ashes of writing (stewing).

If only I could tear this ghastly veil of depression with a laugh! One evening, I take the subway (exhaustion between one station and the next) alone, to Chaillot, to dine with Antoine Vitez between two rehearsals; at the brasserie Le Coq, at the Trocadéro, I order duck: I see the duck, rising from the sauce, flapping its wings and screaming.

How can I follow that fowl to laughter?

I am no longer physically strong enough. If my laughter were the size of my despair, it would kill me on the spot.

Antoine, seeing how I am struggling to think, tells me as he helps me to another serving: *"the more I work on* Tomb...*, the more I think you are a great comic writer."*


In those final days of November, choral music is the only music that I can listen to: since I have ceased to exist, but since my soul has doubled its existence materially, I need the choir to dissolve in it what little existence I have left, and which still shackles my soul; inside the shoulders of singers that press against what remains of mine, inside their heart; to find earthly hope there.

Schumann—the music harking back to the time of my artistic education under my mother's tutelage—wrenches me apart, I can no longer listen to his work. Neither can I listen to the music to which I repeatedly return, the music of enchantment, pleasure, voluptuousness, magic, dream, thinking matter, Debussy, Ravel.

I am obsessed, however by a popular song from the Nivernais or the Charentes, that I recorded a long time ago on the radio between two live takes of wedding music in the desert in El Oued: The Schoolboy Assassin, and I hear it, and hear it again, by day, by night.

*I hear the tranquil song*
*Of the pretty nightingale*

It is the tale of a schoolboy who has returned from Paris to his mother's home. In exchange for laundry and whatever money he desires, she orders him to kill his fiancée: a sword, first, severs the pinkie of the beauty.

*Oh Lord what suffering*
*Must I endure tonight*

Then,

*He lays her on the spike*
*And carves her heart away.*

Our mother never asked as much of me, and yet…?

Some friends accompany me to Chaillot to attend a rehearsal: the main actress, Jany G., takes a fall. From the forestage where I am sitting with Antoine V., with an energy grown violent through exhaustion, I spring toward the stage steps to lift her up.

The only gestures that make me feel that I still have some flesh and bones are gestures toward others: whatever gestures I can have for myself, toward myself, have disappeared.

The night of the dress rehearsal, my friend M., whose father, a hairdresser in Oran, is killed by the OAS in 1962, cuts my hair and gives me a shave.

Following the show, its actions coming to me from afar as if through an abyss, I walk among the guests, a rose in hand; toward a place that I have seen some days before: the two heavy metal sliding doors, bronze perhaps, of a service elevator? Beyond them lies existence, joy. But what I see are the doors on the other side, and on the right, a large, illuminated booth in which young people, girls and boys, celebrate one of their own: crumbs of sugar and of bread, fruit seeds shine on the girls' covered breasts; a boy's upper lip has split down the middle as he laughed and he is licking it in a girl's ear, his hand, emerging from a fur-lined cuff, resting on her breast.

On the night of December 8th, a friend from the neighborhood brings me a bowl of soup; I now sleep exclusively on the cot I have kept from my army days, near the door.

I have a long dream that night, in which Beethoven composes and directs pieces from an unpublished quartet: his warm breath surrounds and envelops my head, steam wafts from the remains of dinner on a back table, musicians, the young inside the half-circle, plump cheeks, the older and graying along the sides, play the almost imponderable, silent music that B. hands them from the piano in large sheets that crackle loudly as they touch.

The image of the scene blurs as I faint on the chair from which I am listening…

My forehead and temples strike the tiled floor, I feel the thrust of my leg muscles from a great distance, my cheek dragging along the tiles, the thud of my skull against the bottom of the door. It is within that dream that I feel myself dying, and an angel marks the ground and the bottom of the door with its imprint (its wing). It is morning.

I shall not be able to open my eyes and move my lips again, at least for the length of a visit or two, until the 13th, the day of the declaration of martial law in Poland, the country where our mother spent her childhood and adolescence; and the following night, in the jolts and starts as I surface to consciousness and sink below— apnea, dyspnea, as if I were stirring, over, under, to one side and the other of a kind of amniotic fluid—the athletic journey begins.

I am in the intensive care unit at the Broussais hospital.

What little is left of my body is strapped to the automatic hospital bed, my nostrils, mouth and other orifices jammed with tubes, clamps... *I* have the bit in my mouth and *I* hear myself from inside the coma snorting like the most robust and furious of horses.

Then, an immense esplanade appears below a range of triangular and shining mountains: cheers rise from several crowds, raving and tossing as if on an ocean floor. Is it *my*self being cheered—but for what?—hoisted upon the fists of one of those masses, or is it someone else, *Rodo*, a lone head standing behind a high platform before me: dark stare and hurried speech? No central voice but four high-pitched cardinal echoes of a ghost of a voice coming out from between his teeth like foam, and drying like a cocoon on his lips.

Is it an effect of what they do to the inanimate object of myself (intubations, catheters, limbs pulled), but the ghosts of what limbs and organs have constituted me on the other side are pulled, quartered as if by the horses at Damien's torture?

Long ago, in childhood, when Summer reverberates and feels and throbs all over, it begins to circumscribe my body along with my self, and my body gives it shape in turn: the "joy" of living, of experiencing, of already foreseeing, dismembers it, this entire body explodes, neurons rush toward what attracts them, zones of sensation break off almost in lumps that come to rest at the four corners of the landscape, at the four corners of Creation.

Or else it is a fusion with the world, my disappearance into all that touches me, all that I see, and into all that I have yet to see. It is hard then to endure being but a single self in the face of all these other selves, and to stay motionless despite the agitation of my senses, to stay motionless in that space where we leap, bound, fly…

Better to die (as a child can "die") than not be multiple, infinitely multiple.

It is such great suffering that we cannot share ourselves, that we cannot be shared like a feast among everything that we wish to eat, among all sensations, among all beings: the shredded corpse of this small animal laying there is me... if it could only be me!

*

A torture den: cries, imprecations, orders, *female*, complaints, moans, pleas that turn to shrieks, to suffocations, to groans; there is scuffling, spillage onto the tiled floor (smells): later, they tell me it is an old woman intubated by the nurses, and who grows slack, and whose feces are shoveled away.

Then, is it the effect of the transfusions and the drip-feed (glucose progressing through my veins) that alters my blood? I am swept into a corridor (veins) of spaces at great speed, thrown into spatial ruins in broad daylight, then the suction pulls me in again.

That pummeling, those slides where I also spin on myself, leave me with something like contusions, aches that I feel in the dream itself—in fact, they are visions, not dreams, for they are too human, they are lived dreams, premonitions, announcements, judgments that seize *me* and deflect *me* back from one time to another;

but toward the origin. The very joints of *my* soul make *me* suffer, they afflict *me*: a jointed soul at the head of a team with its straps, its reins, that *my* arms must drive toward Egypt?

The chamber of echoes again. With a start, the crack of an eye, I see aerosols, tube openings that curve toward me with their rings, serpents, plinth dogs... and enter my mouth, storage depot—but where? the nightstand at the foot of the automatic bed has no tray—for objects, sealed envelopes, *I* am in a tomb in Ancient Egypt with its domestic sculptures, its offerings and messages.

Must I move farther back in time to an era before writing, as if to surprise it from behind, before its hieroglyphs, in its signs, their meaning erased by History, like my own signs whose secret will disappear along with me?

The soul is without a gender, without a species: thus, in this funeral journey, am *I* human, am *I* animal, am *I* god, am *I* object, idea?

I have always seen the gaze of a god staring out from a dog's eyes.

I am the one who wrote that cliché in the *Tomb*: "*like*

*a little dog.*" It torments me, and because of it, I wish—
and have, it seems, enough strength to whisper it to my
friend M. one night—that all I have ever written would
disappear from the surface of the earth.

My punishment is that such an error of art remains.
And *I* am therefore drawn and sinking into an expanse
of columns, of peristyles and of moving draperies, the
raised expanse of a temple-palace around which dogs
await their prey, a long, strong viper of green and gold
whose body hangs along the wall, head facing to attack:
thus, as a child, *I* name "Athalie," queen, obstinately
renegade and wrathful, a viper that hangs from a hole in
our garden wall.

*My* eye cracks open, once again, and the vision of a car-
ton of fruit juice, Rhea, the grip of that mother goddess,
wife of time, takes *me* back by force toward Antiquity,
the "minus" period of the time before the birth of Jesus
Christ: the time of death? That false time before Christ,
that space-time on the edge of which this medical treatment keeps *me* hovering.

The graphs moving upon the monitors of the equip-
ment plugged into *my* heart and brain, before *my* eyes
that part with difficulty, so shrunken have my eyelid
muscles become, draw the trace, the proof of *my* historical

trajectories. Everything, during the year, that *I* have suffered to foresee is accomplished.

Even up to this: that those photographers who have shot
*my* ruined head, which then newspapers have reprinted,
so that *my* kin might gaze on me, in France and beyond,
accompany *me* there—yet do not catch me—like monsters—which they shall remain, for *me*, for a long while
to come.

*

End of December, *I* can sit up on the edge of the bed
with a nurse propping *my* head upon *my* neck. They
transfer me from intensive care to the medical floor
through a tunnel filled with pipes and cables, which runs
beneath a large courtyard illuminated by a large sun. *My*
silhouette rocks like a caricature on the wheelchair.

Here *I* am on the medical floor, housed in the same
corridor, a few doors down from the room where *my*
mother's sister died in late 1979. Across from my bed,
an adult man, pale, with bulging eyes, a shining skull,
eats his meal on his tray. *I* am facing the bottom of a
water hole, of a lake, and that is an amphibian larva
which lies before *me*.

Several hours later my first erection (of what?), between *my* sunken thighs, sets me back into dreadful normality, which the nurse immediately confirms, speaking to *me*: "*Sir,*" "*Mister Guyotat Sir.*"

In February, relocated to the Jeanne d'Arc clinic in Saint-Mandé, my renutrition begins, my skin itches all over because of the flesh forming around the muscles, the cartilages and bones.

After two days of moderate gymnastic activity and writing, the same distress again, but inversely, in a growing body, without that immense deterioration.

On a Sunday evening, the last visitors gone, the intern on duty acts the fool in front of me, and, since I am still struggling to speak at that time, asks me to repeat after him the line from Mallarmé:

*Abolished bauble of sonorous inanity*

Does he think that I have been unable—and will I be able again?—to write so beautifully, so ringingly and melodiously, so despairingly (vanity of sounding soul)—and I, at length!

But he:

*Abolished bauble of sonorous inanity*

So returning to my palate, to my heart and breath the very thing that killed me, the splendor that killed me, that desiccated me, those tempting sounds that brought me beneath its shadow...

After the clinic comes the time to enter into gentle depression, slow healing: instead of the enchanted palace we think we have won by the sweat of our dead blood, the reward for this run through death is a disenchanted world, without notable depth and color, drab gazes that no longer see you, voices always directed toward others since you have returned from too far, a daily obligation to survive, a heart that only pumps blood, and blood that is no longer warming. You must wait. Without anger. Apply yourself daily to eating, to sleeping, to cleaning yourself, to dressing, to walking: all of it, almost alone, and without even yourself by your side: try in jolts, so awkward, to take heart.

Patience, patience,

The End

Afterword by Noura Wedell

# On Translating *Coma*

"At what price, yes, but at what price," Pierre Guyotat tells me from across the table in the coffeeshop in Nation where we meet. I am nerve-wracked, elated to be meeting him, one of the last literary giants, one who *believes*. Sitting across from him means something to me, I cannot abolish that. It is my destiny I am meeting, as he says somewhere in his book. We are talking about a section in the book that I have trouble locating precisely, charting topographically. I ask him simple questions about the layout of the place, a cemetery, a horrible bush, which way to go in order to cross over into the forest past the wall. Is he inside the walls, or outside? Does the tree branch inward or out. I am geographically confused, and think I can latch onto that. I press on with my questions, passing over things, I feel a struggle in the rhythm of our conversation. He wants to settle there a while. Pause. Give it some importance. If I remember correctly, I wasn't even going to ask this question, jumping over the reference to Rimbaud, "j'y suis! j'y suis toujours." ("I am here; I am still here."), because it has become so much a part of our common vocabulary. Well, here we are then, he and I, at the table, and he says that in that moment of his writing, in that moment he is describing in the text: he is there. They were there too, Rimbaud and the others, but Guyotat is there then, just as he is here now sitting across from me. As I myself am here, and you reader.

This new hour is, at the very least, harsh.

For me, the victory is won: the gnashing of teeth, the hissing of fires, the pestilential sighs—all subside. Foul memories fade. My last regrets have cut and run—a jealousy for beggars, brigands, little murderers, the backward and benighted of this earth. God help them if I ever seek my revenge!

I must be absolutely modern.

No hymns! Hold your ground. Hard night! the dried blood smolders on my face; there's nothing behind me but that horrible bush!... Spiritual combat is as brutal as human wars. But the vision of justice never will be ours; it belongs to God, a pleasure He enjoys in solitude.

Meanwhile, this is the eve, the final vigil... Let us welcome, then, an influx of new strength and real tenderness. Come the dawn, armed with our ardent patience, we enter magnificent cities.

Why was I expecting a friendly hand? I have a great advantage; I can laugh at my old, false loves; I can strike those deceitful couples dead with shame. Down there, I saw firsthand the hell of women; and now I'm free to *possess the truth in one soul and one body*.

April–August, 1873[1]

Translating this text has been a struggle. It has been difficult for me to discover this language in English, although it is nothing like Guyotat's other languages (such as the way *Prostitution* has materialized, for example). Here, not only is finding Guyotat's language a struggle, a difficulty that I take on as the regular work of the translator, but it is also hard to beat, to inscribe on paper, metrically. For it is a mixture of classic rhetoric and syntactical liberty, what he calls a "great language" whose normalization cannot hide the live intensity of its rhythm and materiality. And yet my struggle in translation has been nothing compared to withstanding the writer's agony, what Guyotat calls the artistic torment, that is the very matter of *Coma* itself.

---

1. Arthur Rimbaud, *A Season in Hell*, translated by Donald Revell, Richmond, California: Omnidawn Publishing, 2007.

That torment which the self must go through (at least in this description), and be destroyed, to grow to that artistic self, author perhaps but never writer, whose language is an activity just before god.

I myself dwell within the context of the *field*: literature, sociology, politics, extricating and eradicating (or simply observing) what speaks through us of the ideological machine. Information practices, sampling, documentary poetics, technical processes that follow the long announced death of the author and the rise of context. Yet neither are these practices pure formalism. I stand within this context, with its heroines, heroes, great and small: what I can affirm is a belief in the sharing of practices (even though they are hard to perform), the shattering of narcissistic author positions that the institutions of discipline or control and the producers of symbolic capital wield above us as positions of unattainable truth toward oneself (once recognized, then fixed in immutable form, and capitalized upon). We are then nothing but the ersatz of our relation to ourselves, mediated by images, and products. We want that product, truth, destiny.

I say to Guyotat that I am moved in meeting him, so huge is he because he believes. And as we speak of that scene in the cemetery, he repeats that he is there for real, that he is there with literature that has no name. And at what price, he says. I don't know if he would agree with me about belief, for that is no concern of his, as his is not belief, but experience. Talking about the field of literary practices, "le champ," he says he's much more interested in "le chant," the song.

Where I'm from, the song has been broken since Baudelaire with the irruption of the modern, the anti-lyrical. But where Guyotat perseveres is in the trashy purity of the wailing of victims (*Tomb for 500,000 Soldiers*) as they are sodomized, the power beyond the feeling of language as it transforms violence, as it invents itself.

As a child, Guyotat knew he wanted to become an artist. And so he is, and what "the field" (le champ) has told us makes no difference. He has friends in certain circles, of course, no reason to exclude them. And they might help to bring the books into existence. But he also makes friends on the streets, in backrooms, wherever. He is one of our modern day saints.

I will admit it was hard being the body this text passed through, the head, the mouth, the trunk, the hands. It was hard and I loved it. I can reread certain passages time and time again, feel their power, they have an energy that ran through me, running through Guyotat himself to god. A direct running line, impersonal, beyond all narcissistic longing.

It is clearly a physical thing, language and writing. Being a translator is partaking of that pure physicality.

That is why Guyotat writes in the present: the text is a text written in an eternal present. But that is also why he writes in a French form of Latin, with phrases every which way, dismembered across syntax. I have tried, in most cases, to maintain the use of the present, and to provide temporal locators otherwise. I have also tried, within reason, to maintain the Latin syntax in English, and thus to record the stagger of our history as it upturns our speech.

He says to me: you should say that, it would be good to say that.

# LIST OF ILLUSTRATIONS

Some of the images that influenced us as children, my sisters, brothers and I:

Page 23: Freed young deportee in front of a carbonized comrade in *Les témoins qui se firent égorger* (Défense de la France, 1946), photograph by Pierre Viannay. Bibliothèque nationale de France, Paris. Photograph © BNF.

Page 37: Naked Parisian dancer in front of German officers in *Paris sous la botte des Nazis*, autumn 1944. Photograph Roger Schall/Madam R. Schall collection.

Page 49: The young Indian actor Sabu as Mowgli in front of Kaa the python, in *The Jungle Book*, directed by Zoltàn Korda, 1942. Photograph Bifi-D.R.

Page 79: *The Hangman's Tree*, etching by Jacques Callot, from the series *The Miseries and Misfortunes of War*, 1633.

Page 101: Ingrid Bergman as an arrow-struck Joan of Arc, in *Joan of Arc*, directed by Victor Fleming, 1948. Photograph Bifi-D.R.

Page 145: Young, half-naked African woman, in an advertisement for the book, *La France d'Outre-Mer*, in *Historia*, no 88, March 1954.

Page 156–157: Indigenous people from the Amazon, two photographs taken from an article in the journal *Réalités*, 1950s. All rights reserved.

**Other images:**

Page 16: Fra Angelico, *The Martyrdom of Saints Cosmas and Damian*. Detail. Musée du Louvre, Paris. Photograph © RMN-Jean-Gilles Berizzi.

Page 165: *Hallelujah!*, directed by King Vidor, 1929. Photograph Bifi-D.R.

Page 221: The American actress Lilian Gish in *The Wind*, directed by Victor Sjöström, 1928. Bibliothèque nationale de France, Paris. Photograph © BNF.

## ABOUT THE AUTHOR

Pierre Guyotat was born on the 9th of January 1940 in Bourg-Arsenal (Loire). Drafted to Algeria in 1960, he is arrested in early 1962 by military security, in Greater Kabylia, and accused of sapping the morale of the troops, of complicity with desertion and of possession of banned books. He is subjected to 10 days of interrogation and 3 months of secret confinement before being transferred to eastern Algeria as a disciplinary measure. Between 1963 and 1965, he writes *Tombeau pour cinq cent mille soldats* (*Tomb for 500,000 Soldiers*). *Eden, Eden, Eden* is published in 1970, and is banned immediately. *Prostitution* follows in 1975. After *Le Livre* and *Vivre*, 1984, he gravitates toward the theater, producing work for the Festival d'Automne (Bivouac, 1987). *Progénitures* and *Explications* are released in March 2000, *Carnets de bord I* in 2005, *Coma* in 2006 (awarded the prix Décembre), and *Formation* in 2007.